RACHEL HAWTHORNE

DARK OF THE MOON

A DARK GUARDIAN NOVEL

HARPER TEEN
An Imprint of HarperCollinsPublishers

HarperTeen is an imprint of HarperCollins Publishers.

Dark Guardian: Dark of the Moon
www.harperteen.com

Library of Congress Cataloging-in-Publication Data
Hawthorne, Rachel.
    Dark of the moon : a Dark Guardian novel / Rachel Hawthorne.
— 1st ed.
        p.   cm. — (Dark Guardian ; [#3])
    Summary: Seventeen-year-old Brittany was born into a secret
community of werewolves, but when she fails to transform at her
apppointed time, she fears that she will never truly belong.
        ISBN 978-0-06-170957-9 (pbk.)
        [1. Werewolves—Fiction. 2. Supernatural—Fiction. 3. Identity—
Fiction. 4. Forests and forestry—Fiction.] I. Title.
PZ7.H31374Dar 2009   2009014928
[Fic]—dc22   CIP
                                                                        AC

Typography by Andrea Vandergrift
09   10   11   12   13   LP/RRDH   10   9   8   7   6   5   4   3

First Edition

For Gretchen, Kari, and Zareen

Authors are grateful to have one terrific editor on a project.
I was blessed with three. Thank you, ladies, for your guidance,
editing, and enthusiasm for the Dark Guardians.
They wouldn't exist without you.

PROLOGUE

Death hovers in the shadows. Through the slit of the window, the barest of moonlight filters in. I've always drawn comfort from it, but tonight it's Connor offering me solace.

Within our prison, the mound of blankets softens the floor beneath us. One blanket covers us. Connor never bothered to put on the sweatshirt I brought him, so my fingers have the luxury of dancing over his bare chest.

"Don't be afraid, Brittany." Connor's voice is soft, gentle.

But how can I not be afraid? We both know that tomorrow we might die. Facing death brings urgency to

I

life. All the things we've put off, all the things we haven't dared to explore suddenly loom before us as dreams that might never be fulfilled.

Connor holds me close, his warm lips brushing over my temple. Beneath my palm I feel the steady pounding of his heart. How can his be so calm when mine is fluttering like a bird trapped in a cage?

He skims his mouth over my cheek. I hear him taking a deep breath, inhaling my fragrance. I press my face into the curve of his neck and take his unique scent into my lungs. Even here, inside this building where we're held captive, he smells of the outdoors: evergreens, rich earth, sweet nectar, sharp foliage. He smells of everything I love and more.

I've waited so long to know the feel of his hands moving slowly over my back, urging me closer. I never want these moments to end.

"Don't be afraid," he whispers again.

Then the beast inside him that always hovers near the surface breaks free and chases away the gentleness. He kisses me hungrily, desperately as though with our wildness we can ward off the arrival of our enemy. I eagerly return his kiss. I want to experience life with a passion I've never before known. I accept that under normal circumstances we might not be tasting each other or running our hands over each other. But these circumstances aren't normal.

We've been stripped of everything except the intense craving to experience everything we'll soon be denied.

"I love you, Brittany," he whispers.

Tremors cascade through me. My heart pounds against my chest so hard that I'm afraid my ribs might crack. With his words, he's given me what I'd always longed for, what I absolutely don't deserve.

Will his love turn to hate tomorrow when he discovers that I've betrayed him?

ONE

Eight days earlier

Tonight was the big night, the one I'd waited for my entire life. The awakening, the first shift—the loss of my moon virginity.

A few minutes earlier, I'd removed all my clothes. I sat on them now in a small clearing deep in the forest, surrounded by towering trees. Chill bumps erupted along my skin. It was summer. July. But our hidden compound, Wolford, was located in a national forest that bordered Canada. When the sun retreated, the nights grew cool.

Brimming with impatience, I waited. I'd never wanted

anything as badly as I wanted this. Well, except maybe a mate.

But I couldn't help but believe after this momentous night—after I'd proven myself worthy—that the right guy would finally step forward and claim me.

I'd celebrated my seventeenth birthday three days earlier. The first full moon since that day was rising in the night sky. When it reached its zenith, I would transform into a gorgeous creature—into a wolf.

I'd envisioned it a thousand times. I would shed my human shell to reveal what I'd always known resided inside me. I willed it to happen. Even though I knew I should be terrified I wasn't. My fur would be blue-black, just like my hair. My eyes would remain a deep blue. Earlier in the summer, Connor had told me that they reminded him of an ocean surrounded by more ocean. We'd been drinking beer with some campers at the time. I knew his slurred words didn't mean anything, but they'd still given me hope that somehow Connor would become my mate. But the hope had finally shriveled into nothingness, and I focused on the larger picture, the greater good.

For as long as we'd existed, the male of our species had chosen his mate after his transformation and before hers. He went through his alone, but he stood by his mate when she endured her first shift, guiding her so she experienced more pleasure than pain. No female had made the change alone in generations—and the ones who had in the past were considered myths. Legend proclaimed that without a mate, a female faced excruciating pain followed by certain death.

Guess I was about to find out, because no one had claimed me as his mate. The elders, the wise men of our clan, the ones who guided us with their wisdom, had even tried to connect me with someone—Daniel—so I wouldn't have to go through this night alone. I knew they meant well, were trying to protect me, but I didn't want just anyone. I wanted Connor McCandless.

So two nights ago, I'd slipped away from Wolford in the middle of the night. I knew with his sense of smell that Daniel would be able to track me if he wanted to. But I also knew that he was the type of guy who would respect my decision to leave without him. Somewhere out there was the right girl for him, and we both knew it wasn't me.

The first transformation was an intimate, personal experience. I didn't want to go through it with someone who was serving as a stand-in for the real deal, for my true mate. In my heart, it would always be Connor. If I went through this with another guy, I'd feel like I was cheating on Connor. It was an irrational thought because we'd never be together. Still I couldn't control how I felt.

Earlier in the summer, my mom had even offered to

go through my first transformation with me—but that was as creepy as the idea of going to the prom with her. Some things I simply didn't want her to share with me. So I'd encouraged her to take her annual summer trip to Europe. I was fine on my own.

But now as I stared at the yellow orb that possessed more power than humans realized, an uncharacteristic loneliness washed over me. Tonight Connor was with Lindsey because she was going through her first shift beneath the full moon, too. Last summer he'd declared her his mate in front of the entire pack. He believed she was his true love. I wasn't as convinced. Lately, I'd noticed her staring at Rafe. I thought maybe she wanted him, but she'd been promised to Connor, and our traditions weren't meant to be broken.

I couldn't help wishing that Connor had selected me. He had this cute way of using his fingers to comb his shaggy blond hair out of his stunning blue eyes. He was tall, strong, and possessed a body honed to perfection by the constant shifting. Like all male shifters, he was predatory and dangerous. Totally hot.

Not that I was into Connor because of his physical prowess. It sounded stupid to say I loved his mind, but I was into the way he read situations, considered strategies, and never jumped into Shifter mode at the first sign of trouble. He weighed options.

I just wished his heart had been as cautious before he'd announced Lindsey was his mate. Following the ancient tradition, he had a Celtic symbol representing her name tattooed on his shoulder.

I fought not to think about Connor and Lindsey standing together wearing only the ceremonial cloaks reserved for mates preparing for their bonding. I'd heard that going through a transformation together was an incredibly soul-binding experience. That it wasn't only the moonlight that caressed, that touched, that whispered—

Groaning, I banished the haunting images. I would suffer enough tonight without thinking about them and the attraction that would pull them into each other's arms.

I lifted my gaze to the star-filled sky. The moon that guided our destinies was high overhead. I should start to feel something at any minute.

As a rule, no one ever discussed their first transformation. It was as private as the loss of your virginity. But I'd felt as though I had no choice but to seek advice on what to expect. So I'd spoken with Kayla, who had survived her first shift during the last full moon. She'd told me that it had felt as though the moonlight was actually touching her, coaxing her beast to reveal itself.

Concerned that I'd be going through this alone since no guy had ever shown an interest in me, I'd been preparing all year. I'd built up my stamina by running every morning. I'd strengthened my muscles using weights. I'd disciplined my body for this incredible moment. When my beast burst forth, I'd tame it, gain control of it. I could hardly wait.

If I survived, I'd move into the realm of legend. I would confirm that guys weren't the only ones who could survive going through this alone. That idea was so sexist anyway. Let's move into the twenty-first century already. Our kind had some really archaic customs. But I was seventeen, liberated, ready to embrace my destiny. Even if that destiny didn't include Connor.

I closed my eyes and imagined how it might have been if he was here. We'd be standing so close that the breeze wouldn't be able to pass between us. He would cradle my face with his large hands. Very slowly he would move in to kiss me. We wouldn't rush the moment. Then his lips would brush over mine as a deep growl rumbled up from his chest. His beast would call to mine and mine would answer with a softer sound. We would embrace, riding the wave of pleasure and pain, and then we'd transform together.

Thoughts of him not connected to Lindsey brought me comfort as I waited. If I pretended I wasn't alone, maybe I could conquer the pain that would soon envelop me.

Why didn't it come—while I was prepared to face it?

Before the doubts I'd been holding at bay began to creep back in?

The ability to transform was mine by birthright, passed from parent to child through our DNA. But as my time had drawn near, I'd begun to have disturbing dreams. In them, I stared at the moon, waiting for it to keep its promise. But it, not me, shifted. It became the sun and I remained human.

Kayla had said that she could sense the change coming long before her birthday, before she even knew she would have the ability to transform, but I'd felt nothing. When the caterpillar is enclosing itself in a cocoon does it know that it'll emerge as a butterfly?

I *knew* that I would emerge from this night as a wolf, but I didn't *feel* it. Fear gripped me. I felt the way I'd always felt, like a human, like a Static—our derogatory term for those beings who didn't have the ability to shift.

But I was a Shifter. My parents were Shifters. I'd grown up surrounded by Shifters.

I tried to will the change to come, but tonight the moon called the shots. After that, I'd be able to change at will. But for now, I had to tamp down my impatience, and that was almost impossible. I wanted so badly to be a full-fledged Dark Guardian. They were the protectors of our kind. Knights. The ones who handled any ene-mies who might want to attack us. Right now we had an incredibly dangerous enemy threatening to destroy us and the time for the final confrontation was quickly approaching. I wanted to be in the thick of it.

I wanted to cast off my novice status. Tonight that would happen. Once I shifted.

I opened my eyes. The moon seemed lower in the sky. But that couldn't be. I hadn't noticed any tingling. Maybe it had happened without me feeling anything, but when I looked down, I was still human. Still a girl. Not the wolf I'd always envisioned I'd be: the wondrous creature that lived deep inside me.

No, no, no.

Maybe I needed to be standing. I jumped to my feet and outstretched my arms toward the sky. I wanted to call out to someone, something—

I heard a distant howl echo through the night. The voice was one I'd never heard before. Was that Lindsey?

No! This absolutely couldn't be happening. I wouldn't let it happen.

I ran as though I could catch up with the quickly disappearing moon, as though I could somehow . . .

What? Touch it? Make it reach its zenith again?

I crumpled to the earth and felt the hot tears coursing down my cheeks. It wasn't fair. But it was what I'd always feared. Why else would Connor look at me and not see his mate? Why else wouldn't he know that I was his destiny? Why had he settled for stupid Lindsey?

I'd always felt that something was lacking in me. I had always felt as though I was on the edge of everything, the outsider desperately wanting to be accepted by the clique. Oh, people acknowledged me, but there was always a distance. *Don't get too close, Brittany. You're one of us, but you're not connected to us. The girls will talk to you, but never confide in you. They will befriend you, but never invite you into their most intimate inner circle. Our males will fight beside you, but never be drawn to you.* No one, no one had ever asked me out on a date. No one had ever kissed me. No one had ever looked at me with heat in his eyes.

Did I not change because a guy wasn't with me? That made no sense. It was the moon that changed us. The moon that called us.

I bent my head back and howled—

But it wasn't the cry of a wolf. It was the anguished shriek of a girl. A human.

A human whose soul was cracking and whose heart was breaking.

I wasn't a Shifter.

I, Brittany Reed, was nothing.

TWO

I didn't remember falling asleep. My last memories were of me screaming until my throat was raw and my fists pounding the earth until my hands ached. But exhaustion must have claimed me at some point because I woke up and stared at the sunlight dancing over the leaves.

I'd always loved the wilderness, but suddenly I didn't feel one with it any longer. I thought I could hear the trees mocking me as their leaves rustled in the breeze. I didn't know where I *wanted* to go, but I knew where I *needed* to go. I had to return to Wolford. The Dark Guardians were gathering there, in order to figure out how to protect our—*their*—kind. Bio-Chrome, a research company, had discovered that we existed and was determined to uncover the secrets of our—*their*—ability to shift, even if it meant killing us—*them*.

I gave myself a hard mental kick in the butt. I had to stop thinking such divisive thoughts. It wasn't them—the Shifters—versus me, the non-Shifter. It was *us*. Sure, something had gone wrong, but that didn't mean it couldn't be fixed. I had to keep my mind open to the possibility that it was some fluke of nature that could be easily corrected. Maybe my birthday was too close to the full moon and I needed another cycle to prepare my body to shift. Maybe the date was wrong on my birth certificate. God, I was really grasping at straws, wanting desperately to find an easy answer.

I knew I couldn't tell anyone that I hadn't yet shifted. I'd waited too long, worked too hard to finally be accepted. I didn't want to face that I might not be a Shifter. There was another reason that I hadn't transformed. Whatever it was, I'd figure it out.

Grabbing my nearby backpack, I headed out. I'd planned to lope toward the compound, embracing my new self, the wind ruffling my fur. Instead, I trudged through the forest, forcing my feet to move along, one in front of the other. An explanation for what *hadn't* happened had to exist somewhere. I considered discussing my situation with the elders. They were so old that they knew everything. But I didn't want anyone to know the truth about me.

If they did discover the truth, they'd look at me with pity or horror. We existed alongside humans, but none of us wanted to be like them. They were pitiful creatures, Statics, always locked in the same form. They might even cast me out. I couldn't take that risk with danger lurking. I was a Dark Guardian. It was all I'd ever wanted to be.

How was I going to look at myself the first time I gazed in a mirror, the first time I saw what I truly was— or wasn't?

Because I was afraid the elders might send Guardians out to search for me, I took a circuitous route back to Wolford. I needed this time alone to shore up my courage to face everyone and not give anything away. It wouldn't be easy for me. I wasn't someone who believed in sugar-coating things. I was known for being honest and facing the reality of situations. Facing my own reality was going to be a bitch.

Few people had truly embraced me before. If they learned that I couldn't shift, they'd view me as a freak of nature. It was bad enough that I'd received the occasional odd stare because no guy had claimed me as his mate. I didn't want to have to endure the others knowing that I hadn't shifted on time.

It was nearly noon on the second day when I ran

across the cold remains of a campfire on the banks of one of the rivers that ran through the national forest. My heart galloped as I knelt and sifted the ash through my fingers. I detected no heat at all, and I hadn't noticed any light in the area when I'd bedded down the night before. It could have been several days since anyone had been here—but it felt more recent. I couldn't explain why I had that sensation.

The fine hairs on my arms prickled as I gazed at the rapidly flowing river. It was possible someone had been rafting and pulled over here to set up camp for the night. Farther down the river was a series of tight curves and turbulent white water. It was great for sports enthusiasts, but they were usually accompanied by a guide who would turn them back before they traveled this far north, this close to Wolford.

It seemed paranoid to have a bad feeling about what I'd discovered, but I couldn't help sensing that something wasn't right. Very slowly and cautiously, I walked around the camp, noting the various boot prints that had been left behind. I could identify four distinct sets. It was also obvious that they'd arrived and left by the river. I discovered a groove in the bank where their rubber raft would have scraped along the ground as they pulled it onto shore.

On the opposite side of the camp, I noticed an area

where it looked as though evidence of prints had been brushed away with a leafy branch. The brush marks stopped near dense foliage. Grabbing a large stick, I began poking it around the brush. I heard the snap as I triggered a release mechanism that I'd suspected was hidden in there. The stick was jerked from my hand as the noose closed around it and the rope swung it up in the air, until it dangled high above my head, the branches shuddering with the force of being set loose.

A snare trap. One of the simplest traps to set. Still dangerous. Still capable of killing an animal—but it was also possible the animal would survive being slung around as it was lifted from the ground. Judging by the setup, it had been designed to capture a medium-sized animal. Not a rabbit. Not a bear. But a wolf.

A cold shiver raced down my spine as I backed away. I'd bet my life that I knew who was responsible. It wasn't game hunters, sportsmen, or survivalists.

It was Bio-Chrome. Our enemy. They were stepping up their efforts to capture a Shifter and they were getting closer to discovering Wolford.

I had to get back quickly. I had to warn them. And I hoped I wasn't too late.

I felt a sense of relief when I finally arrived at Wolford to see the main residence still standing. I saw no evidence of violence. Nothing seemed out of the ordinary.

Because I'd originally been two days away from Wolford, and because I'd been dragging my feet in no hurry to get back—until I discovered the trap—it was nearly midnight the next night when I finally reached the wrought iron gate that surrounded the compound. A couple of hundred years ago, most of the Shifters had lived here, hidden away from the rest of the world. But as the world had begun to change with modernization and industrialization, they'd moved out among humans—benefiting from and contributing to achievements. Still this forest remained our true home—the one place where we could be ourselves and celebrate what we were.

I slipped a keycard into the slot and the gate clicked open. It seemed strange to me that we were a combination of the old and modern. We used keycards for access, but we still believed in the ancient ritual of guys declaring their mates. Go figure.

After walking through, I stood there while the gate clanked shut, its sound reverberating through me. I'd always found solace here. No enemy had ever penetrated our walls. Here, tradition was passed down from one generation to the next. Closing my eyes, I took a deep breath and tried to draw in the calm of my ancestors. But I felt unwelcome, as though I were a stranger or worse, a fake.

I wished my mother was here. I didn't often need her. I'd always wanted to be independent, so it was difficult now to admit that I yearned to have her arms around me. I'd felt relief when she'd left for Europe because I'd known she wouldn't be around to interfere. I hadn't thought I'd be able to put up with her hovering and worrying. I loved Mom, but she was a hoverer. Always trying to protect me. I'd become somewhat rebellious just to break free of her emotional restraints. I knew she meant well, but sometimes I felt as though she were smothering me.

As for my father, he'd always been a no-show in my life. Apparently he'd seen my mother through her transformation, hung around long enough to knock her up, then taken a hike to parts unknown. She had managed quite well without a man in her life—which was the reason that I'd been convinced that I hadn't needed a guy for my transformation.

I walked toward the massive mansion that was pretty much all that remained of what we'd once had here. Oh, there were a few buildings around that held supplies and various survival items, but when our kind visited Wolford, they stayed in this mammoth Gothic-like structure where families had once enjoyed a communal-like existence. It had been refurbished to include all the modern conveniences. Our elders lived here throughout the year.

Hidden away in the national forest, it provided us

with a sanctuary. The Dark Guardians worked as forest guides—otherwise known as sherpas—and kept people away from the secret areas of the forest that we considered off-limits to outsiders. Although really, we considered the entire forest as ours, even though the government had claimed part of it.

Out of the corner of my eye, I caught movement and dropped into a defensive crouch, my actions honed by hours of survival training. To my surprise, I saw Connor heading toward a thick copse of trees in the distance. Although his back was to me, I recognized his loose-hipped stride. He walked as though he was never in a hurry to get anywhere. The moonlight reflected off his sandy blond hair and outlined his well-toned body. He was tall and slender, but I knew he possessed the strength of all Shifters. We not only hid our ability to shift, but the power that came with it. Looking at us, few people realized how strong and capable we were.

As Connor disappeared between the trees, I wondered why he was alone. Where was Lindsey? Usually a couple became totally inseparable after they shared a shifting. Could there possibly be trouble in paradise?

I wasn't exactly sure how I felt about that. As much as I'd wanted Connor to notice me, to claim me, and go through the transformation with me, I didn't want Lindsey to treat him badly. Neither did I want him to hurt Lindsey. She was a friend. I selfishly wanted Connor and unselfishly wished them the best. My confused and contradictory feelings left me unsettled. As a rule, I usually knew what I wanted.

I glanced around quickly. No one else was in sight. I should let Connor go, but I'd never felt so alone or devastated in my life. I needed to connect with someone. Why not him? Just for a few minutes. It wasn't like I was going to ask him to cheat on Lindsey. I had standards. I didn't steal another girl's guy—but that didn't mean I couldn't talk to him and get my Connor-fix.

After hiking since the full moon, I was gritty and dirty. Normally I would have taken the time to clean up because I never wanted Connor to see me at my worst, but I didn't want to miss this opportunity to talk with him alone. Maybe because even though he didn't feel a connection to me, I felt one to him. I was pathetic to be crushing on a guy, knowing he cared for someone else, but at that moment, I couldn't quench my desire to hear his voice.

I tossed my backpack toward the side of the house and raced in the direction I'd last seen Connor. The dew-covered grass left a clear trail, but once I hit the woods, he wasn't as easy to follow. The grass wasn't thick around the trees and the moonlight filtered in sparingly between the leaves. If I'd shifted, I'd have been able to capture his scent and follow it. All senses heightened after the first transformation. Shifters acquired keen night vision and enhanced smell, hearing, and taste. Even their skin became more sensitive.

All I had to go on was my gut instinct, so I simply kept moving forward and hoped he'd done the same. He might not be my mate, but we were friends. And right now, I needed a friend. Desperately.

The woods were never totally quiet at night and I drew comfort from the familiar sounds. The insects chirped. An owl hooted. I heard some tiny creature, probably a rodent, stirring up the dried leaves that coated the ground. But I couldn't hear any footsteps other than mine. I wondered if Connor had shifted, if he'd taken off. But I didn't see his clothes lying around.

The trees finally gave way to a brook where the shallow water splashed over rocks, creating nature's lullaby. Standing at the bank's edge, as still as a statue, was Connor.

My heart gave a little lurch, the way it always did when I first got near him. Sometimes when we were packing up supplies, getting ready to guide campers out into the wilderness, our shoulders would brush and it was like an arrow zinging through me, from shoulder to toes. Insane, I know, to be so affected by his nearness. It hurt that we'd never be more than friends, that he would forever belong to someone else.

If I was smart, I'd turn around, head back to the mansion, and get on with my life. Obviously I didn't possess an ounce of intelligence because I strode forward until I was standing beside him. He didn't look at me. He just kept staring at the water.

I had so much that I wanted to tell him, so much that I couldn't explain, things I didn't want him to know. Still, a calmness settled over me as I studied the outline of his familiar profile in the moonlight. His features contained a ruggedness that I associated with warriors. The strength in his jaw line was almost obscured by his shaggy blond hair that hung down to his collar. I wanted to run my hands through it. I desperately wanted to loosen my braid and have him comb his fingers through the heavy strands of my own hair. I wanted to press my face into the curve of his shoulder and have his strong arms come around me. I wanted so much that I couldn't have. I didn't know if I'd be strong enough to settle for friendship now that I knew he was totally and completely beyond my reach.

"Guess you heard," he finally muttered, and I heard the hardness in his voice.

Connor was seldom quick to anger, but I'd seen his fury when we discovered that human scientists working for Bio-Chrome had found out about our existence and were determined to use us for their own gain. Connor believed we'd somehow come out victorious, that life could miraculously return to normal. Or what was normal for us.

But now his anger-laced words caused horrible scenarios to rush through my mind. Had Bio-Chrome captured Lindsey? Was the trap I'd discovered only one of many? Had they killed her? Was that the reason that Connor was alone? Was he in mourning? Or had she not transformed? Had something been wrong with the moon? For the first time in days, I grasped tightly to a miniscule of hope that the full moon—and not me—had been the aberration.

"Heard what?" I asked quietly.

Then I noticed the white bandage peering out beneath the sleeve of his T-shirt. We didn't often sport bandages. In wolf form, Shifters could heal amazingly fast—unless the wound had been inflicted by silver or the bite of another lycanthrope. Then the process took forever and left a scar. Our healing abilities were one of the things that made us attractive to Bio-Chrome. Even in the heat of battle only the worst of wounds could slow us down, because we continued to heal, providing us with a living sort of armor.

"You're hurt," I whispered, and in spite of my best intentions, I reached out and trailed my fingers near the bandage. I felt his firm muscles quiver and ripple beneath my touch. I'd never deliberately touched him. His skin was smooth and warm. I wanted to know the feel of his face, his neck, his chest . . . I wanted to know what everything about him felt like.

"Rafe." He said the one word as though it should explain everything.

Rafe was a Dark Guardian, part of our pack, part of our sherpa team. He was as dark-haired, as dark-complexioned as me. He'd grown up with us, fought beside us against our enemies. He was as loyal to our kind as any of us. "Rafe bit you?"

Connor snorted, and I could sense the anger now rolling off him in waves. "I bit him back. Wish I had rabies. It would serve him right."

"I don't understand, Connor. Where's Lindsey? What happened?"

"Rafe challenged me for her."

"What? You mean wolf to wolf?" A challenge was never made lightly. Tradition had it that when one wolf challenged another, it was a fight to the death.

"Yeah."

"Oh my God! But you're her mate. You declared her; she accepted you." It was always the girl's right to not choose the guy who had declared her his mate. But I'd never known it to happen. "You've been together for as long as—"

"Yeah, well, apparently I chose wrong."

He continued to look forward, as though he were embarrassed, or maybe he just didn't want me to see in his eyes the depth of his rejection and loss. I knew he was hurting. It was evident in every muscle of his body. He'd always loved Lindsey. Would it make him feel any better if I told him that I loved him? I didn't think so. I couldn't replace what he'd thought he lost.

"I'm sorry." And I was. This was exactly what I'd always wished for, but now that it had happened—I felt guilty, as though my wishing for it had somehow made it happen, had brought him this pain.

"Not your fault. It's just the way it is, but it's still hard to swallow, you know?"

"I know."

He turned his head to look at me directly. Even with the moonlight I couldn't see the blue of his eyes that were a shade darker than mine, but what I could see surprised me. He wasn't sad. He looked as though he was disgusted with himself. Then he shook it off, as though he didn't want to reveal so much. What replaced it surprised me even more. I saw admiration. "I see you survived your full moon. I can't believe you took off on your own. That took guts. I mean, no one has ever doubted your courage, but what you did went above and beyond."

Guilt gnawed at me because he was praising me when

I so didn't deserve it. I wanted to tell him the truth. The burden of what I was—or wasn't—was so hard to bear but I was afraid he'd be appalled by the reality of what I was. How could he not be?

We had never, ever, allowed a non-Shifter into our inner circle. Standing there I was confused about what I truly was: a Shifter who somehow the moon had passed by but would return for later or someone who would never be anything more than she was at that precise moment.

If it was the latter, what was the point in existing at all? How could I protect the Shifters if I wasn't one of them? But I couldn't turn my back on them either.

I eased away from him and stared at the water, the way the moon reflected off it and made it prettier than it was during the day. "It was no big deal." Especially since nothing happened.

"Hey, like all guys, I went through it alone. It's brutal."

"I don't want to talk about it. It was a totally private experience."

"Got it."

I didn't know why I was disappointed by his response. I guessed I wanted him to care enough to prod the truth out of me.

"Did you know Lindsey liked Rafe?" he asked.

"She mentioned him a couple of times." It had always

irritated me when she did. If Connor had been mine, I'd have never even looked at another guy. My voice had a hard edge when I said, "I never thought she appreciated you. You're better off without her."

He barked out his harsh laughter. "Typical Brittany. You're never afraid to say what you're thinking. I've always admired that about you."

If I'd died right at that moment, I would have died happy. Connor had admitted that he admired something about me? Me? I felt like smiling and laughing when I hadn't thought I'd ever again feel like doing either. I wanted to tell him that there was a lot about him that I liked and admired but the moment wasn't right.

While I didn't say anything, silence settled in between us and other communication was going on. We were gazing into each other's eyes, and I wondered if he was seeing me—truly seeing me—for maybe the first time. He seemed lost in thought—and I wished I could read his mind. I tried not to let my eyes reflect the depth of feelings I held for him. I was still a little too vulnerable from the moon's betrayal to risk my heart with Connor at that moment. But I wasn't afraid to meet his gaze, to hold it. Then his gaze dropped to my lips and they began to tingle. Was he thinking about kissing me?

As much as I wanted him to, I didn't want him to kiss me until he was over Lindsey. I wasn't going to serve as a rebound girl. Still, I seemed unable to stop myself from licking my lips, from anticipating a kiss, from imagining how warm and wonderful it would be.

As though coming out of a trance, Connor gave his head a little shake before he dropped it back and stared at the night sky. "I need to run." His voice was raspy, sexy. He cleared his throat. "So, do you want to run with me?"

Oh, I wanted to, desperately. But I knew he wasn't talking about jogging through the forest. He was talking about shifting and running so fast that the trees would become a blur.

"Facing the full moon alone took a lot out of me," I said. That much at least was true. "I'm going to pass."

"Another time then." He looked back at me. "I remember when I faced my first transformation. I couldn't wait, but I also remember the pain. The elders would have found someone else to go through it with you if you didn't like Daniel."

"They drew his name out of a hat." I didn't bother to hide my disgust.

"It wasn't like that. They used a bowl."

I pounded my fist into his shoulder.

"Ouch!" He rubbed his arm, but he was smiling.

"It was insulting—to me and Daniel." He wasn't a bad guy, but he wasn't the right one either. We'd spent a few days together, but we'd both known it was a lost cause. "I didn't want a pity mate."

"You've got the wrong attitude about it. It's not like you had to marry the guy. He was just supposed to help you get through it. Nothing more."

Except for the whole getting-naked part. We couldn't transform in our clothes. So there was a definite intimacy factor. "It's all moot now. The pressure is off. I can choose a mate anytime."

"It'll never be like the first time you shift."

I shrugged. "As far as I'm concerned, the first time is overrated."

His grin flashed in the night. "Well, don't tell anyone. Don't want to ruin the mystique for the others who haven't yet experienced it." Something shifted in his eyes that I couldn't quite identify. "I'm glad you survived."

"Yeah, me, too." Sorta. And then I remembered what I'd seen near the river. "Hey, listen, has anyone mentioned finding traps in the woods?"

"No. Why?"

"I ran across a snare about a day and a half walk from here, near the river."

He got really still, the way a predator does when it scents its prey. I knew he'd gone into warrior mode, was considering strategy.

"You think it was Bio-Chrome?" he finally asked.

"I don't know. Maybe. It was designed to capture something the size of a wolf."

He released a harsh curse, then gave me a hard stare. "You walked from there? You didn't think you needed to travel in wolf form so you could get here more quickly?"

"I had my backpack with me." I knew it was a lame excuse, which Connor confirmed with his next words.

"You could have left it somewhere, gone back for it later."

It made me angry that he was questioning me—also that he was right. And that I'd had no choice in my mode of transportation. Two legs were all I had access to at the moment, so I searched for another lie. "I'd taken some sentimental items with me to help me face the transformation alone. I didn't want to risk losing them. Besides, it wasn't as though we were in immediate danger, and I needed the time alone."

The tightening of his jaw only confirmed for me that no one would accept me if I couldn't shift. I also realized that lying about it wasn't going to be easy either. I should have come up with a better excuse—one that didn't make me look irresponsible.

"I'll check it out," he said. "In wolf form, I should be able to get there and back by morning. Are you sure you're not up to coming with me?"

How I wished . . .

"I'm sure. I covered my tracks, but you should be able to follow my scent."

I could tell he wasn't happy with my decision, that he thought I was shirking my responsibilities. By not telling him the truth about me, I was. But my fallacy—whatever had prevented me from shifting during the full moon—was mine to deal with.

"Later then," he said grudgingly.

Turning on his heel, he walked back into the forest, but I didn't follow. I knew he was going to remove his clothes and transform into a wolf. For a species that spent a lot of its time without clothes on, we were a modest group.

Looking back out over the water, regrets prodded me. I knew that I should confess my limitations, but I also knew that if I did, I might be cast out. But even without the ability to shift, I could still make a valuable contribution, could find a way to protect the Shifters—especially if what I suspected was true: The trap was set by Bio-Chrome. They were still coming after us.

Nothing was left for me to do right then except return to the mansion. I couldn't go with Connor into the night. He was free now to love someone else, but I was shackled by my inability to shift.

Hearing the rustling of brush, I glanced to the side. The most beautiful wolf I'd ever seen stood at the water's edge. In wolf form, Connor always took my breath.

His fur, like his hair, was a sandy blond that bordered on light brown. It had various shades, darker along his back, lighter near his paws. I wanted to dig my hands in his fur, hold him close, and confess everything. I wanted him to shift back into human form, put his arms around me, and assure me that everything would be all right.

But I knew none of that would ever happen. If he knew the truth about me, that I hadn't shifted yet, he'd be appalled.

With a last look at me, he splashed across the brook and loped away, awash in moonlight. With longing, I watched until I could no longer see him. Shifters healed when in wolf form, but I wasn't sure that shifting would heal a broken heart—either his or mine.

THREE

As I hurried back to the main house, I realized that I now had something I hadn't had before: a chance with Connor.

And just as quickly reality slapped me hard in the face. That chance was only available if I could figure out what had happened to me, why I hadn't shifted. I mean, really, what guy wanted a Static girlfriend?

When I arrived at the house, I located my backpack, started for the front door, and stopped. It was late. Only a few lights were on, but I wasn't ready to run into anyone else and continue with my cover-up. Besides, I had something I wanted to check.

We were an ancient civilization. Some believed we'd been around since the dawn of time. Others thought we'd come into existence with King Arthur and the magic of Merlin that had surrounded him. The elders never really confirmed our origins. They simply protected the secrets of our history. Those secrets were housed within ancient texts that the passage of time had made so fragile that only the elders were allowed to read and study them.

While I walked in the shadows along the side of the house, heading toward the back, my mind drifted to the ancient texts that were stored in a room that only the elders were allowed into alone. They'd shown the room to the Dark Guardians, reverently removed the ancient book from a glass box, and allowed us to touch the worn leather so we'd have more regard for our past. But the book was never opened in front of us. The words were never read to us. Surely something so carefully guarded contained secrets—and answers.

I didn't bother sneaking. No point when the night guards had a keen sense of smell. I was surprised that I hadn't spotted anyone yet, but I figured they were probably on the far perimeter. Their job was to stop anyone who shouldn't be here from getting this close. They weren't here to stop us from doing anything *we* shouldn't. After all, we'd all sworn an oath to be honorable. An oath I was about to break.

When I reached the back door, I turned the knob—not surprised to find it locked. I swiped the keycard and watched the red blinking light turn green. Taking a deep breath, I slipped inside and quietly closed the door behind me.

Now was the time for stealth. I was in an area we were discouraged from hanging out in. The hallway was unlit. Closing my eyes, I envisioned what everything had looked like when the elders brought us to this area of the residence. The hall was wide. Tables decorated with antiques and statuettes honoring wolves lined the walls. If I simply walked down the center, I should be okay.

I crept slowly and carefully, until my eyes adjusted to the gloom and the shadows began to take shape. I realized that a few of the doors were open. Pale moonlight spilled through the windows into the rooms and whispered into the hallway. But it wasn't an open door that interested me.

My heart thundering, I came to a stop in front of a closed door. I knew if I was discovered I'd be stripped of my Dark Guardian status—but that was going to happen anyway if I didn't get some answers. I put my hand on the knob and a chill went through me. I wasn't certain if it was the knob or my hand that was cold. It was as though the ghosts from the past were breathing down my neck.

"Enough already," I muttered. Squeezing my eyes shut, I twisted the knob.

It opened.

I bit my bottom lip to stop myself from gasping out loud with surprise. I wasn't sure what I was expecting. Or what I thought I was going to do if it hadn't opened. Was someone in there? Was one of the elders working late? Or did they trust us to respect that we weren't supposed to enter this room? Or maybe someone had just forgotten to lock it.

Pushing on the door, I cringed when the hinges gave a *creak*. I glanced around quickly, then decided the hell with it. I shoved open the door and stepped inside.

No one was there.

I switched on the light and dimmed it. An ancient mahogany desk sat in front of a massive fireplace. The mantel was stone with feral-looking wolves carved into it at either end. I guessed that they symbolized Dark Guardians watching over the treasures. The room was huge with ornate brocade chairs and carved wooden chests scattered throughout. I could envision the elders sitting around and going through the treasures tucked away in the chests for safekeeping. Leather-bound books lined the shelves on two of the walls, but those weren't the books I was interested in. The one I cared about was in the glass case on a stand in the corner.

I set my backpack in a chair. Striding by the desk, I grabbed a stone paperweight, fully prepared to do whatever was necessary to get at that book. I'd worry about the consequences later. I knew I was being rash, but I was also desperate. But when I got there, I saw no lock, only hinges. Could it be that simple? That unprotected?

Carefully I lifted the glass lid. A breath of relief rushed out of me. I could do this without leaving any evidence behind. Setting the paperweight aside, I reached in and closed my fingers around the ancient tome. It felt as though it weighed a ton as I lifted it out and carried it to the desk. Carefully, with respect, I set it down. Taking a deep breath, my heart pounding so hard that I couldn't hear anything except for the blood rushing between my ears, I very slowly turned back the cover.

And stared at the indecipherable symbols.

Had I truly believed that an ancient document would be written with modern letters and words?

I turned to a page at random. More garbage.

I wanted to scream! I wanted to tear out the pages, I wanted to destroy—

"Oh my God, you're back!"

With my heart leaping into my throat, I jerked my head up to see Lindsey standing there. She was dressed in shorts and a tank, her long blond hair flowing around her shoulders. She looked different. More confident, more mature, more . . . wolfish. Before I could respond, she rushed across the room and hugged me tightly.

"I've been so worried," she said.

I wanted to lash out at her, shove her away, but at the same time I wanted to draw her closer, absorb the comfort that she didn't even realize she was providing. I knew she'd acquired what I'd so desperately wanted. Did she even appreciate what it was to shift?

With her brow furrowed—no doubt because of my less-than-enthusiastic greeting—she leaned back and studied me. "Are you all right? Was it horribly painful?"

More than you can imagine.

I rolled a shoulder as though I couldn't be bothered. "No biggie."

"I thought the pain was going to kill me."

"You were always a wimp."

"Not anymore. I'll show you my fur later if you'll show me yours," she said teasingly.

God, I wanted to weep and I never cried. It made me mad that I was changing but not in the way I'd expected. I fought to keep my voice calm, noncommittal. "We'll see."

Then the significance of her words struck me. "Wait. You were with your mate. I didn't think it was supposed to hurt."

"For a while I wasn't with my mate." She licked her

lips, suddenly looking uncomfortable. That made two of us.

"Rafe is my mate," she blurted.

"So tell me something I don't know."

"You already heard?"

I didn't want to tell her that I'd seen Connor earlier. Just like my inability to shift, my few moments of connecting with him weren't meant to be shared. Besides, they probably had only meant something to me. By tomorrow he will have forgotten our talk by the brook—except for the part about the snares. Anything intimate, though, would be long gone. "No, but Rafe has that whole looking-at-you-like-you-hang-the-moon-and-stars thing going. I knew you were going to end up with him."

"Wish you'd told me. I was so confused, but now . . . I don't know how I could have ever thought he wasn't the one." She shook her head. "Still, I feel bad about Connor. He deserved better."

Yeah, he did. But I wasn't here to give her grief or question her decisions. She and Connor had been friends for most of their lives. I knew it couldn't have been easy for either of them to suddenly find themselves needing to go in separate directions. I'd been giving her a hard time all summer because I didn't think she and Connor were right for each other. But that was over. We had to move forward.

Lindsey glanced around suspiciously now that the

thrill of finding me alive had worn off. "Brittany, what are you doing here?"

I met her gaze, the guilt gnawing at me. "Nothing."

She looked down at the thick leather-bound book. "That's the ancient text. What have you done?"

"I just wanted to read about our origins," I said.

"Without permission? That's a sacred book, the only copy we have. Only the elders have the right—"

"To hell with the elders."

She stared at me. "Brittany, we should leave."

"Not until I have answers." Maybe there was an English translation somewhere—on the shelves or in one of the chests.

"Is it about finding your mate?" Lindsey asked.

I released a brittle laugh. And then the impact of her words hit me full force. Gave me hope. "Oh God. Do you think that's what it was? Do you think it's because I didn't have a mate?"

"What are you talking about?"

Damn it. I couldn't stop the tears. They were warm going down my cheeks. I didn't want to, but I had to tell someone. I had to share this horrible disaster. Lindsey and I had been friends for years. She was the closest thing I had to a best friend. "I didn't transform, Lindsey. Nothing happened."

She simply stared at me. No words of comfort, no

reassurances. But I respected that she wasn't trying to lie to me.

"Are you sure?" she hesitantly asked, her voice quivering with the unease she couldn't control.

I glared at her. "It's kind of a hard thing to miss."

"I thought maybe you passed out or something. We can retain our shape if we're sleeping, but not if we're unconscious."

"No, pain wasn't the issue."

She looked as though she might be ill. She wasn't the only one whose stomach was roiling. Gingerly I touched the brittle parchment. "I thought maybe there was something I was supposed to do, some ritual to perform, some words I was supposed to say."

Lindsey shook her head. "I don't think so. I mean, I started to feel it, like, almost all day. My skin got really sensitive."

"I didn't feel that. I didn't feel anything at all. What's wrong with me, Lindsey? Why didn't I transform? Is that why no one claimed me? Because all the guys could sense that I'm a freak?"

"You're not a freak," she insisted. "A lot of people can't—"

"They're not us. They're not like us!" I clamped my mouth shut. The fear and the horror of what I was needed its own voice. It didn't even sound like me yelling.

Lindsey looked as calm and cool as always. She couldn't truly understand the frustration and disappointment I was feeling. She had it all: the guy she loved and the ability to shift.

"This is unheard of—someone not shifting. You have to talk to the elders," she said. "They'll know what to do."

She lived in such a dream world. "No, they won't. And I don't want anyone to know. I shouldn't have even told you."

"I won't tell anyone, but, Brittany, someone will figure it out. I mean, shifting—it's what we do. You should at least tell Lucas."

Lucas was our fearless leader, the one in charge of the Dark Guardians and our pack of young wolves. Earlier in the summer, he'd connected with his true mate, Kayla. They were madly in love. That was the way it was supposed to happen with us. We were supposed to be willing to die for the other person. I wanted that level of commitment. I shook my head. "How could this have happened?"

"Maybe they made a mistake on your birth certificate. Maybe your birthday is wrong."

Despite the fact that I'd clung to that hope briefly, hearing Lindsey say it out loud made me realize how ridiculous it was. "Get real. You think my mom doesn't know when my birthday is? She was kinda there, you know?"

"Okay, so that was a desperate search for a reason—but there has to be a reason and someone, one of the elders, will know what it is," she said.

Angrily I wiped away my tears. I didn't want her sympathy. I didn't want her trying to solve my problem. I'd always been independent, taken care of myself. "I'm being such a girly-girl. The next thing you know, I'll be wearing pink."

"Nothing wrong with pink."

"I'll figure it out. Maybe I'm just a late bloomer. Yeah, that's probably it." Closing the book, I gave her a wry grin. Our relationship had been strained for most of the summer—mostly because of how I thought she was being unfair to Connor. But there had been more. Just an underlying sense that she'd been changing in ways I hadn't. I'd sure gotten that right. "I'm sorry I've been so difficult lately. I just haven't felt like myself. And I've felt even less like myself since the full moon."

"That's okay. You were right about me and Connor. My feelings for him weren't as intense as they should have been and it totally wasn't fair to him. He could probably use a good friend right now. Based on how worried you were that he was making a mistake with me, I got the sense that you really like him. I'm not standing in the way now."

"Why would he want someone who can't shift?"

"Two wounded souls?"

I couldn't help myself. I smiled at that. "God, you're so Romeo and Juliet."

"What would it hurt? To just talk with him, I mean?"

I already had, but again I didn't want her to know. "I don't know. Maybe. Promise me, on your sacred vow as a Dark Guardian, that you won't tell anyone about me."

"I won't." She made an X over her heart. It was a childish gesture, but it actually brought me comfort. "Cross my heart. Besides, it could just be a temporary glitch. Maybe you need another moon cycle."

I wanted to believe that's all it was. I glanced around. "What were you doing lurking around this hallway anyway?"

"Taking a shortcut to meet Rafe. He's out guarding the perimeter and getting a little lonely."

"You should go then if he's expecting you."

"Yeah." She took a step back. "Are you going to be okay?"

Nodding, I sniffled. "Yeah. Whatever the reason, I'll find it."

After she left, I put the book back in the glass case. Using the edge of my shirt, I wiped away the prints, not that it would probably do any good. If the elders came to this room anytime soon, they'd catch my scent.

I spent the next half hour going through books and papers. Most were written in a language I didn't read. Those that weren't were original works by Shakespeare or Dickens. They wouldn't help me. I finally decided that I wasn't going to find anything in here of value to my personal dilemma. I took a last look around. Nothing appeared disturbed.

Switching off the light, I stepped into the hallway and closed the door behind me, feeling as though I was closing the door on something else more important: my future as a Dark Guardian.

FOUR

The ominous silence followed me up the stairs to the room I shared with Kayla and Lindsey. In a way, I wished I'd come here immediately and faced Kayla and Lindsey at the same time—instead of taking my detour with Connor. Kayla would have the same questions. I just needed to be stronger this time and keep my horrid secret to myself. As quietly as possible, I opened the door. The room was dark except for the moonlight coming in through the window. But there was a presence, a charged electricity—

"Brittany?" I saw Kayla's shadowy silhouette popping up in bed, and suddenly light flooded the room as she switched on a lamp.

I didn't try to hide my surprise at the sight of Lucas rolling into a sitting position, pulling his T-shirt over his head. I knew now what I'd felt when I first walked into the room: steamy passion. Lucas combed his fingers through his hair, while Kayla slipped the shoulder of her tank top back into place.

"Uh, aren't there rules against this, even between mates?" I asked lightly, hoping that by joking they wouldn't sense something was wrong with me. Only married mates were allowed to share a room. It was a little comforting to know even our leader didn't follow rules.

Kayla was blushing when she scrambled off the bed and came toward me. "Lindsey left and it's so hard to find time alone . . . Lucas just got here. Honest. If we'd known you were coming back tonight"—she shook her head—"I've gotta have a hug first and then I'll apologize."

Before I could respond, she flung her arms around me. "We've all been so intensely worried about you, afraid you wouldn't survive. Lindsey especially. Lucas and I were just talking about sending out search parties tomorrow."

"Yeah, I'm sure you guys were *talking*," I teased, as I hugged her tightly, needing the support if not for the reasons she thought.

"We were, in between kisses," she assured me.

When we broke apart, I forced a cocky smile and shrugged. "Don't know what the big deal was. It wasn't nearly as bad as everyone implied it would be."

I was grateful Lucas was there. If he hadn't been, I might have dropped my guard and told Kayla the truth. Her joy over my return had taken me by surprise—I hadn't expected her to be so worried or so glad to have me back safe and sound. It made me wonder if maybe I'd misjudged how much she cared for me. In some ways it made it more difficult because if I *was* part of the inner circle, it was going to be more painful if I lost that sense of camaraderie.

"Still, I wish you would have let someone go with you. I mean, you just left, headed out without telling anyone. The elders were a little freaked," Kayla said.

I couldn't imagine the elders getting freaked about anything having to do with me—or anything else for that matter. They were always impossibly calm, as though excitement had long ago left their lives. I looked over at Lucas. "Thanks for not sending anyone to follow me."

"Figured if you wanted someone with you then you would have taken someone," Lucas said.

"Appreciate the show of confidence." I really wanted to change the subject and I needed him to know what I discovered. "You should know, on my way back, I ran across a snare."

Lucas went all still, the same way Connor had. "Bio-Chrome?"

I bit my lower lip. If I'd shifted, my sense of smell would have been heightened enough that I would have known for sure. "I think so. I saw Connor before I came inside. I told him about it. He's gone to check it out."

Lucas nodded with obvious satisfaction. "Good. He'll get to the bottom of it."

He ambled over, giving me an intense once-over as though he was looking for tufts of fur. "You sure you're okay?"

So much for thinking a change in subject would stay changed. "Absolutely. Why wouldn't I be?"

He arched a dark brow, because I was being stubborn. "I don't think any she-wolf has gone through it alone, at least not in recorded history. The elders are probably going to want to talk with you."

Great. That's just what I want.

"I'll be around," I said more easily than I felt. I decided one more time to end the subject. "It's done now." After tossing my backpack on the bed, I pointed at each of them. "And you two are done as well."

Kayla wrapped her hand around my arm, the way people did when they were going to deliver bad news and thought the person hearing it might need to remain standing. "When you saw Connor, did he tell you about Lindsey and Rafe?"

"Yeah."

"Big surprise, huh?"

"Not totally." She and Lindsey were tight. I liked Kayla but I didn't feel a sisterhood bond or anything. I wondered how much of that had to do with whatever was messed up in my Shifter genes. "Last summer when you met Lindsey, you felt an immediate connection, didn't you?"

Kayla had been adopted by Statics, raised away from Shifters. Last summer she'd returned to the forest—our forest—where her birth parents had been killed.

"Yeah, I did. It was kinda weird, but comforting at the same time." Giving Lucas a soft smile, she blushed. "Although I'll admit the connection I felt to Lucas scared me."

"Why?"

"It was like getting hit with a baseball bat or something. I was thinking about him all the time. I wasn't sure he even liked me."

"What's not to like?" he asked, slipping his arm around her and drawing her up against his side. That he was crazy in love with her was written all over his face. I figured the only reason they weren't playing tonsil hockey was because I was standing two feet away. Time to make my exit.

"I hate to be a party pooper, but I'm tired and grungy," I told them. "I'm going to hit the shower and then bed.

Don't steam up the room while I'm gone."

Lucas grinned wolfishly. He'd always been so dark and brooding that it was strange to see this lighter, almost teasing side of him. Even with all our troubles, Kayla could make him smile.

"I'll wait up for you," Kayla told me, "and we can catch up some more."

"Not necessary."

She gave me a funny look. I wasn't usually this anti-social, but neither was I the buddy type.

"I'm just really tired," I told her; even though she hadn't asked I could see the question in her eyes.

Before I started making more excuses and maybe raising suspicions, I went to the bathroom, closed the door, and stared at my reflection in the mirror. I looked the same. Even knowing that I would, I was still disappointed.

But so far I'd passed the inspection of three Shifters. If I could fool the ones I worked with and saw every day, I could fool anyone. Maybe even myself.

The next morning, with my head buried beneath my pillow, I mumbled something about needing more sleep when Lindsey and Kayla were getting dressed, so they'd leave without me. I didn't want to have to endure any more scrutiny or questions.

When I went down for breakfast, the dining room

wasn't crowded. It was large enough to accommodate families when we had our annual gathering. Now, only the Dark Guardians and a few Guardians-in-training were hanging around Wolford.

I saw Kayla and Lucas sitting at a table alone. She caught my eye, smiled, and pointed to an empty chair beside her. I shook my head. Lindsey and Rafe were also at a table alone, but they were lost in each other and not paying attention to anyone else. Ah, newly discovered love. They had a lot of lost time to make up for. A few other Dark Guardians—those who had faced their first full moon and novices who were still anxiously awaiting their magical night—were scattered throughout the place. They smiled at me and gave me a thumbs-up. I'd survived. I'd made it. Yay me.

I walked to the sideboard where the buffet breakfast was set out. I heaped scrambled eggs, bacon, and toast onto my plate. Then I sat at a table by myself. I wasn't up to answering questions about how my transformation had gone.

Too bad I hadn't sent out a mass email alerting people to back off.

Three novices were suddenly surrounding my table. Mia and Jocelyn were sixteen, Samuel seventeen. Guys didn't have their first transformation until they were eighteen.

"You did it!" Mia said, fairly bouncing on her toes. Her blond hair was short and feathered in little delicate wisps around her elfin face. She was the only Shifter girl I knew who didn't keep her hair long. "Do you know what this means for the rest of us? We don't have to choose our mate before the transformation. Your courage has given every girl freedom!"

My courage? Was she kidding me? I hadn't been alone because I *wanted* to be. I was alone because the only guy I'd been interested in was interested in someone else at the time.

"How bad was it really?" Jocelyn asked hesitantly, and I knew it was because she was aware that Shifters didn't openly discuss the first transformation with someone they weren't tight with. It had a mystique.

Jocelyn's reddish brown hair hanging straight down her back reminded me of autumn leaves. She and Samuel had their fingers laced together. He'd claimed her during the summer solstice when our kind always got together to celebrate our existence. She wasn't going to be going through it alone.

I looked back over at Mia. Would I be condemning her to death if I made light of things? I truly had no idea how bad it might be.

"I thought I was going to die. I don't recommend going through it alone." At least I'd spoken the truth.

Mia's jubilant face fell. "But you survived."

"Just barely." I felt mean saying that but what choice did I have? I didn't want her death on my conscience.

"But if I started to prepare like you did—"

I cut her off. "You've got another year. You might have a mate by then." Hadn't Lindsey said almost the same words to me, trying to reassure me that I'd be okay? I hated being deceitful. It was only a few days ago that I had been making the same arguments as Mia. But now I knew better. Or, at least, that it wasn't that simple.

"I think it's archaic that we have to have mates," Mia said stubbornly, jutting up her small chin.

"Gee, thanks, Mia," Samuel said. "Some of us like the traditions."

"And some of us don't. Look at all the technology we have. Get with the program."

"Enhancing our security using technology has nothing to do with how we should uphold our traditions."

"It has everything to do with it."

"Guys, now isn't the time," Jocelyn said with obvious irritation as though she'd been forced to sit through the debate a thousand times. She smiled at me. "We just wanted to stop by and talk to you. We think you're awesome. It would be kinda creepy to just . . . touch you, wouldn't it?"

The next thing I knew they'd be auctioning my

crumpled napkin on eBay. "Definitely creepy."

With a last nod at me, they walked away, laughing and tittering, and glancing back as though they still couldn't believe that I was breathing the same air as they did. There were so many ramifications to what I'd done that I hadn't given any thought to most of them. Who would have thought that anyone except me would have cared that I went through it alone? And how was I to know that by lying about all that had happened, I'd suddenly be carrying a heavy responsibility on my shoulders?

I was a Dark Guardian. I was supposed to protect these people. I should stand up in my chair, get their attention, and announce the truth of what had happened. I was debating the pros and cons of that action, considering how mortifying it would be, when a shadow fell over my plate. My heart hammering, I jerked my gaze up, hoping to see Connor. Instead I saw Daniel, the guy with whom the elders had tried to set me up. He gave me a warm smile. I smiled back. No hard feelings. He was a nice guy, but we'd both accepted from the get-go that we weren't going to make it as a couple.

He set his plate on the table and pulled out a chair. "Glad to see you didn't need me after all," he teased.

"Everyone keeps looking at me like I'm a freak." Or maybe that was just my imagination because I knew I was one.

"You're a legend. Although I have heard that a few guys are worried that the need-a-mate myth might be challenged by other girls."

"Yeah, I got a taste of that a few minutes ago when some of the novices stopped by to drool over me. Honestly I don't know whether to be flattered or appalled by the idea that I may start a trend."

"Most people would relish the limelight."

"I'm not most people."

"You'll get no argument from me about that. So how was it really?"

"Probably the same as it was when you went through it." I was becoming quite adept at spinning things and avoiding giving direct answers to questions.

"Terrifying, but awesome?"

"Exactly. So what's been going on since I left?" I asked, anxious to change the topic.

"Not much as far as I can tell. In case you haven't heard, Lucas called a meeting to bring us up to speed. We're to head to the council room as soon as we're finished with breakfast."

Daniel began talking about some of the things they were learning about Bio-Chrome, the company that had researchers trying to capture and study us. I was only half listening. I'd been part of the sherpa team that had led them into the wilderness earlier in the summer before we knew their objective. I knew all I needed to know about them. Mason Keane and his father—who was in charge of the project—were certifiably insane.

As Daniel's melodious voice droned on—he was apparently unperturbed by the fact that I wasn't an active participant in the conversation—I didn't know why I hadn't taken more of an interest in him. Like most male Shifters, he had a raspy voice—the better to growl with. He was the only Shifter male I knew who wore his hair buzzed close to his scalp. Which I thought was a shame because his eyes were an emerald-green that I thought would have looked stunning framed by his black hair. His face was animated as he talked, and I knew he couldn't wait to confront the bad guys. But I just couldn't concentrate on him.

Maybe because I was acutely aware that Connor had arrived. Even though I couldn't see him. I was experiencing the kind of sensation that wild animals did when they sensed a change in the environment and all their senses went on even higher alert. The flight or fight response. Usually we fought. My awareness of him gave me hope that maybe I *was* simply a late bloomer.

As nonchalantly as possible, I glanced over my shoulder. Connor was at the sidebar, filling his plate. I wanted to watch him. Even the way he scooped eggs was sexy. I wanted to know what he'd discovered when he went searching for the abandoned campsite. I wondered if I should invite him to join us. Before I could decide, he strode past and settled at an empty table.

Ouch! I tried not to grow concerned that in following my trail, he may have also somehow detected that I hadn't shifted.

I turned my attention back to Daniel, but I felt Connor's gaze homing in on me. The hairs on the nape of my neck prickled, but in a good way, causing my fears of discovery to dissipate. My hair was arranged in its usual no-frills, long braid, because today we'd be tending to Dark Guardian business. Part of me wished that I'd worn it down, but going for the feminine look had never been my style. I was all about projecting a tough image, even when I didn't feel very tough. Maybe that was another reason that guys didn't flock around me.

I didn't want to be rude, so I tried to concentrate on Daniel. But I was very much aware of Connor studying me. Even though he wasn't doing anything except eating, he kept drawing my attention like a magnet. Whenever my gaze shifted over to him, he didn't look away. If anything he appeared irritated. Was he upset that I was enjoying breakfast with Daniel? Or was he still angry about being the first Guardian in generations to lose his mate? But if that was it, why was he looking at me and not Lindsey?

Daniel launched into a funny story about some

campers he'd recently guided into the forest, making me laugh. I discreetly observed Connor out of the corner of my eye. He was scowling. He did look away then, and I felt this strange sense of triumph. Could he be jealous? My heart gave a small unexpected leap at the idea.

There were other Shifter girls waiting for the arrival of their full moon who would need a mate. Would he turn to one of them, or was he sensing the same thing I was: an inescapable connection, as if there were a rope bridging us, tautening and pulling us together. Was he as confused by it as I was?

My gaze drifted back over to him. I'd always liked him, but his attention had always been on Lindsey. Now that he no longer had a destined mate, was he finally taking notice of me?

"And then the squirrel ran up my leg searching for nuts."

I nearly spewed my coffee and my eyes went wide as I jerked my head around to stare at Daniel.

He gave me a wry grin and chuckled. "I thought that would get your attention."

"I've been listening."

"No, you haven't." He gave a meaningful nod in Connor's direction. So much for my subtle observation. "But I can't blame you for wondering about Connor. We're all wondering."

"Wondering what?"

"What exactly happened with him and Lindsey and Rafe—out there in the woods, during the full moon. None of them are talking."

"It's not really anybody's business, is it?" My words came out tarter than I'd meant for them to, but I didn't like people gossiping about my friends. "Sorry," I said quickly. "Didn't mean to snap at you like that, but well—"

"I know. You're a team. It creates a bond. I shouldn't have said anything."

Lucas, Kayla, Rafe, Lindsey, Connor, and I *were* a sherpa team. We usually worked together to lead campers into the forest. But our bond, our friendship, went beyond that. Although Kayla was new to our group, the rest of us had gone to school together. Daniel had just moved here from the Washington State area. They had Shifter sanctuaries out there, but everyone wanted to be skilled enough to be selected to protect the Wolford area. It was, like, the capital of the Shifter world—at least the North American contingent.

"Would you feel better if one of our best guardians was dead?" I asked. While the challenge should have meant a fight to the death, we'd evolved, become more civilized. Surely.

Daniel blushed. "Okay, I get it. Not my business.

Anyway, I'll see you at the meeting."

After he left, I looked back to where Connor had been sitting. The chair was empty. It was silly of me to feel a sense of loss, but I did. Even my appetite had abandoned me.

I took my tray to the kitchen and headed out. In my rush, I nearly rammed into Elder Wilde. He was Lucas's grandfather. The Wildes were almost like royalty. For generations, a Wilde had served as our pack leader, always passing the position down to the eldest son. Lucas was an exception, but no one questioned his leadership after he fought his older brother for the right to lead us.

Elder Wilde's surprisingly strong hands dropped down on my shoulders like lead weights. I nearly stumbled from the surprise of it. "Brittany, I'd sensed that you were back."

Smelled me more like it, but he was too polite to say.

"The other elders and I would like to have a word with you in the treasures room."

Great. I couldn't run. Even though he was old, when he was in wolf form he could outpace and outdistance me. I couldn't hide. He'd sniff me out.

So I did the only thing I could do. I swallowed hard and nodded.

FIVE

The Council of Elders was made up of three. They didn't look all that bad considering they'd each been around for at least a century. They weren't immortal, but the aging process was slowed by their healing ability. Still, Shifters do eventually age, and they were showing the signs. A little more bent, a little more withered and sporting manes of snowy white hair.

But their eyes were sharp, and damn it, their ability to scent probably was, too.

We were sitting in chairs near the fireplace. I felt as though the snarling wolves on the mantel were looking directly at me, passing judgment.

The elders studied me. I fought not to show any nervousness and prayed they wouldn't ask me to demonstrate my ability to shift. It hadn't occurred to me until that moment that maybe we had to reveal our wolf form to them before we could shed our novice status. That was going to be a bit of a problem. I also realized that if Shifters possessed some sort of instinctual connection with one another—something like what Kayla had sensed with Lindsey—that the elders might also be able to tap into the fact that I hadn't shifted. But if that was the case, wouldn't they confront me about it?

I tried not to envision how it would go—the distrust they might exhibit.

"So," Elder Wilde finally said.

I arched a brow. "So?"

He gave me an indulgent smile. "In all of our history, there is no record of a female surviving her first transformation alone."

"There has to be a first time for everything, right?"

"Was it painful?"

"Like you wouldn't believe." I gave a self-conscious laugh. "I guess you would believe. You went through it, right?"

They all smiled. At least they'd retained their sense of humor.

Just don't ask me to shift. Please don't ask me to shift.

"We still believe it's important that you find a mate," Elder Wilde said.

Relief swamped me. If they were still trying to set me up, then they had to be sensing that I was a Shifter. So what had gone wrong? Would they have the answer if I confessed the truth? Would they decide I wasn't up to being a Dark Guardian? With Bio-Chrome still a threat, I wanted to do what I could to protect Shifters. Even if I couldn't yet shift, I truly believed that I could help, could make a difference, could have an impact.

I nodded quickly at his belief that I needed to find a mate. "Oh yeah, definitely. I'm totally up for that. I just want to do it at my own pace."

"We were thinking of sending you to various other sanctuaries. We have them throughout the world. It could just be that, like your mother's situation, your mate isn't *here*. She found hers in Europe."

My jaw dropped. I snapped it back up. My mom had never told me that little tidbit. I'd always assumed he was someone from around here. Was that the reason she went to Europe every summer? To be with him? Why hadn't she ever told me? More importantly, why didn't she take me with her to meet him? Maybe she wasn't going to see him, maybe she was just trying to find him. Mom had always been so mysterious where my dad was concerned, like maybe she was ashamed of him or something. But then why wouldn't she be? He hadn't hung around.

But as stunning as the revelation about my mother was, I was more concerned with what he was suggesting for me. "I don't want to leave here, especially now with"— Connor no longer tied to Lindsey—"Bio-Chrome threatening us. Our very existence could be in jeopardy."

"I told the others you would feel this way," Elder Mitchell said. "You've always been one of our most loyal novices."

"Definitely. I feel very strongly about this. We have to protect the pack. At all costs." Even if that cost was lying until I understood what had happened to me. "Don't send me away."

"It's not a punishment, Brittany," Elder Wilde said. "It can be very lonely when everyone around you has a mate."

"The pack comes first."

Elder Wilde sighed as though I were suggesting something that would land me in detention. The elders looked at one another, arched brows, nodded. I knew that in wolf form, Shifters could read one another's thoughts. I had a feeling the elders could do it when they weren't in Shifter mode. I hoped they couldn't read mine. Just to be safe, I fought to make my mind blank.

"You won't find anyone more loyal than me," I blurted. "Let me prove it."

"We don't question your loyalty," Elder Wilde said. "We want what is best for you."

"Staying is best for me."

They did another round of head nodding.

Finally Elder Wilde sighed as though he'd lost the argument. "We're in agreement. We need you while the Bio-Chrome threat is here. But destiny chooses our mates. If your mate is elsewhere, it's not fair to you—or him—for us to hold you here forever."

I could have told them that he wasn't elsewhere. There was obviously a defect in me that wouldn't cause that instant bonding. I was going to have to secure a mate the human way—by making him fall in love with me.

Good luck with that, Brittany.

I was more than ready to leave and decided my best course of action was to initiate the ending of the meeting. I tapped my watch. "Lucas is calling a meeting of the Dark Guardians. I should probably go."

Elder Wilde smiled. "One more question."

I nodded expectantly. They hadn't been too hard so far.

"Did you find what you were looking for in the ancient book?"

Okay, I should have expected that. I felt all the air leak out of me like a balloon. I considered denying it, but even I thought I could smell my scent from last night lingering in here. Although that was probably just in my head or guilt making me sense things I couldn't possibly sense. I shook my head.

"Would you like to share with us what you were seeking? Maybe we can be of assistance."

"It's really not important enough to bother you with."

I expected them to question whether it was important enough to break rules over, but instead, Elder Wilde studied me quietly, giving me the impression that he knew *exactly* what I'd been searching for. I expected him to admonish me, or torture me, or make me confess the truth of my situation.

Instead, he simply said, "Well, you are right about our needing to get to the meeting. Your first as a full-fledged Dark Guardian. Should prove interesting."

I kept my expression passive, even though I was stunned. That was it?

As I rose to my feet, Elder Wilde said, "Remember, Brittany, deception may give us what we want for the present, but it will always take it away in the end."

For a minute, I thought he was sharing something he'd read in a fortune cookie, but then I realized he was way too serious.

"What are you talking about?" I asked nervously. Did they know the truth?

"May you never find out."

As I followed them out of the room, I couldn't help but feel that I was being tested in some way. But the greater test was Bio-Chrome. I knew I could help the Dark Guardians defeat them—but only if I was a Guardian.

If I didn't shift during the next full moon, then I'd confess everything to the elders, ask for their guidance and assistance.

But for now, I was determined to be what I'd always longed to be: a Dark Guardian.

When we arrived at the council room, I hung back, respectfully waiting for the elders to take their place at the large round table that occupied the center of the room. Twelve additional chairs circled it. Eleven Guardians were standing behind their chairs. Kayla stood on one side of Lucas. Rafe, his second-in-command, was on the other side of him. Lindsey stood so close to Rafe that light could barely filter between their shoulders. Her fingers continually touched his, and then retreated, as though she couldn't stand the thought of not having some skin-to-skin contact with him, but knew it was inappropriate here in the council room. Her golden eyes were focused on me, as though I were the only one in the room. They were imploring me to speak up, to reveal my ugly secret, to release her of the burden of truth she carried on her shoulders.

Sorry, Lindsey. No can do.

The chair between Connor and Daniel was empty. Staring at it, knowing it was designated for me, I swallowed hard. Every meeting before this one, I'd sat in a chair along a wall, the place designated for the novices. A Dark Guardian who hadn't yet been caressed by a full moon. The significance of this meeting slammed into me. I was finally qualified to sit at the big table. Or so they all thought.

I knew I needed to move forward but my feet felt as though someone had super-glued them to the floor. More than moving forward, I knew Lindsey was right. I needed to confess my deep, dark secret. I knew I did. I knew it was wrong to place my butt in a chair that rightfully belonged to a warrior. I needed to just suck it up, accept the reality of—

Lucas grinned at me, his silver eyes teasing. "Come on, Brittany. I don't know anyone who's wanted—or deserved—this moment more than you."

So true. No one else put in the hours working out like I did. No one else ate as healthily—and boringly—as I did. Chocolate hadn't passed between my lips in years. I'd wanted to be the best Dark Guardian ever. No reason I couldn't be. I was smart and strong. I'd trained in the martial arts. I knew this wilderness as well as I knew every feature of Connor's face. I'd willingly die for the Shifters—without hesitation or regret.

What did it matter if I hadn't yet shifted? I'd been prepared to pull my weight before my full moon. My devotion, my readiness hadn't changed.

With a deep breath, I strode forward to stand behind the empty chair beside Connor. Dark blond bristles shadowed his face as though he hadn't bothered to shave since the last full moon. His hair was combed back in its usual style but looked as though he'd merely used his fingers rather than a comb to arrange it. He'd never looked sexier. As wrong as it was, I drew strength from his nearness, as though I could actually feel the warmth of his body reaching out to mine.

With a scraping of chairs over the stone floor, everyone took a seat.

Connor leaned over and I caught a whiff of his unique earthy scent. "Welcome to the big table," he whispered in a low voice.

Holding his blue gaze, I fought not to grin like an idiot, not only because I was sitting at the big table but because he was there beside me, acknowledging me. "Thanks. How's the arm?"

His eyes hardened and I realized *that* was not exactly the best conversation starter. I should have gone with, "What did you discover out there about the snare?"

"Healed," he said curtly, and whatever camaraderie might have been developing between us came to a screeching halt. He turned his attention to Lucas.

Because I could feel Daniel studying me, I smiled at him. He gave me a thumbs-up. He really was a nice guy. We just didn't have any chemistry.

"As most of you know," Lucas began and I directed my attention to our leader, "we recently found a lab that Bio-Chrome had set up at the northeastern edge of the forest. They captured Connor, Kayla, and me—but we managed to escape with help from Lindsey and Rafe."

I slid my gaze over to Lindsey and Rafe. His hair was as dark as mine, but that was where our similarities ended. His eyes were brown and so full of adoration for Lindsey that I was stunned to realize how much inner strength it must have taken for him to keep all those emotions hidden away. But was I really any different when it came to what I felt for Connor?

We believed in destiny, that our mates were kindred souls. I shifted my gaze over to Connor and it collided with his. My heart slammed against my ribs with the intensity of his stare. Was he watching me so closely because he was suddenly interested or was it because he was beginning to sense that I didn't belong at this table?

Soul mates were supposed to be able to decipher each other's thoughts. Could I even afford to have a mate now? Or would my thoughts always be locked away from other Shifters?

"Then on the way back to Wolford, Brittany came across a snare," Lucas announced.

I heard a couple of sharp intakes of breath as the other Guardians turned their attention expectantly to me. As much as I wanted to lie about it, I knew doing so would put Shifters in danger. "I don't know if Bio-Chrome set it," I admitted.

"They did," Connor said. "I checked it out last night. Picked up a scent."

Panic caused my stomach to flutter. How was I going to explain why I hadn't picked up the scent? Was I going to have to come clean about what hadn't happened during the full moon?

"Mason's?" Kayla asked. She and Mason had been friends earlier in the summer before she discovered what they planned for the Shifters.

"No," Connor answered, before meeting Lucas's gaze. "It was the scent of one of the mercenaries Bio-Chrome hired to help them find us. I figure Brittany didn't recognize it because she wasn't with us when we were captured."

I fought not to reveal how relieved I was with that explanation. When they'd been captured, I'd been with a group of girls camping in the forest.

"I found three other snares," Connor continued. "They followed the river. I didn't find any evidence of them scouting nearby, but it's just a matter of time."

Lucas nodded. "Good work, Brittany."

Normally I enjoyed praise, but I felt like a fake accepting it for something I'd simply stumbled across. "I just got lucky."

"*Lucky* Bio-Chrome wasn't around," Daniel muttered.

"So what are we going to do about the lab?" I asked.

Lucas gave me a patient smile. He, too, was dark, but his hair was a medley of colors: brown, black, silver, white. It made him a very easily identifiable wolf to humans. "Best case scenario: We destroy the lab, but that's tricky. We can't burn it without risking the forest. Even though it's not located inside the national forest itself, it's still surrounded by trees. A fire doesn't respect property lines. But we do know a Shifter who owns a company that implodes buildings for demolition. I'm going to meet with him. See what he recommends."

My granddad, my mom's father, had once taken me to watch an old hotel being taken down. It was in the middle of a city, buildings all around it. They'd reduced it to rubble without damaging anything else in the vicinity. It had actually been pretty cool to watch.

"Don't suppose it's too much to hope that their lab geeks will be inside when it goes down," Connor said.

"Do we want their deaths on us?" Lucas asked. "That's something we have to think about."

"If all we do is destroy the building, they'll just build another one somewhere else—maybe one that's more difficult for us to get to," Connor pointed out. "And they'll still come after us."

"Maybe we should out ourselves," Kayla said.

A bold comment from someone who'd only just discovered that our kind existed.

"I don't know that the world is ready for that," Lucas said. "Could just bring us more trouble."

"I say, bring it on," I stated emphatically.

Beside me, Connor chuckled and I had another one of those feel-good moments when I thought maybe if I could make him completely forget about Lindsey that I might have a chance of hooking up with him.

Lucas looked toward the elders as though seeking their counsel.

Elder Wilde stood. "It is possible that the time has come to reveal our existence to the world, but it is not a decision that can be made in haste. And it will carry consequences. We cannot forget how we were persecuted in the ancient world when our existence was known. Well-trained hunters were charged with destroying us. We went into hiding for so long that our kind is only remembered as a myth. We cannot deny that the world has since changed, but has it changed enough to accept us? We cannot yet say, but we will take your suggestions under advisement." He sat and folded his hands on top of the table as though to signal he'd finished.

Lucas turned his attention back to us.

"When do you anticipate we can take action?" Rafe asked, and I felt Connor stiffen beside me. I admired him for not growling. I couldn't imagine how much courage it took for him to be here, knowing that everyone in the room had expected Lindsey to be his mate. Our kind had rituals. For Lindsey to be with Rafe, everyone would know that Rafe had challenged Connor—and Connor had lost.

I hadn't considered that before. I'd always thought they were well matched. Would Connor have thrown the fight intentionally? I hadn't thought to ask last night. Since it was supposed to be a fight to the death—well, someone had shown mercy. I wanted to believe it was Connor.

"I'm thinking that our best chance for success will come during the dark of the moon," Lucas said. "We have night vision on our side."

"And they have night-vision goggles," Connor pointed out.

"Possibly. But a moonless night will give us the best chance of cover."

Connor nodded, as though he reluctantly agreed.

"Okay then, I'm going to divide us into smaller teams.

Some of you will stay here at Wolford, some will scout the forest searching for any more signs of Bio-Chrome, and another team will head to the lab. For now you can all relax. I'll post assignments later this morning. Tomorrow we get to work. Are there any questions?"

I glanced around. Everyone appeared determined. Tension radiated on the air but I sensed it was because we were all anxious to protect our kind.

"All right, then," Lucas said. He then nodded toward Elder Wilde, relinquishing control of the meeting.

Elder Wilde stood. "You all carry a heavy burden. We've always turned to our youth for protection because you're stronger, hungrier, more eager to prove your worth. But wisdom comes with experience. If you need counsel, come to us." His eyes fell on me and I fought not to look guilty. "We are here to serve and guide. But you are our guardians from the darkness that can be humankind. Go forth." He moved his hands in a widening circle, giving us permission to leave.

As everyone started to get up, I took my time, trying to think of something clever to say to Connor. I felt a tug on my braid and looked over at Daniel.

He smiled at me. "You're one tough Dark Guardian."

"Thanks."

I didn't have to look to know that Connor had moved on. I strongly felt his absence. I was a mess: hopeful one moment, facing reality the next. Sooner or later a situation might arrive in which I would have to shift. What would Connor think of me and my deception then? Was I simply delaying his inevitable disgust? If he fell in love with me, would he forgive me? Or would he simply hate me all the more?

Lucas called Daniel over to where he, Connor, and Rafe were talking. I figured he was about to send them out on patrol.

"Maybe we can catch up later," Daniel said.

I nodded. "Yeah, sure."

After he walked off, it occurred to me that I needed to introduce him to one of the novices or something. He was new to our area and he needed to expand his circle of friends to more than just me.

I was in the hallway when I ran into Kayla.

"So what did the elders want?" she asked.

"To send me away."

"What do you mean? Like, back to Tarrant?"

Tarrant was the small town near the entrance to the national forest. Most of us had grown up there.

"No, I mean, like to other forests, other areas, places where other Shifters hang out. They think my true mate is out there somewhere just waiting to connect with me."

Her jaw dropped. "Are you serious?"

"Yeah. Whoever heard of matchmaking grand-fathers?"

"Maybe they're worried about keeping the species thriving."

I shook my head. "Nah, I think they just finished their Sudoku puzzles for the day and were bored, so they decided to meddle."

"Maybe they care about you."

She made me feel guilty for having unkind thoughts about their attempt to play Cupid. From an early age, we were taught to respect them. But who wanted to be set up by men who'd probably forgotten what it's like to first fall in love?

Looking over my shoulder, I could see through the doorway and into the council room. Connor, Lucas, and Rafe seemed to be engaged in an intense discussion. I had no doubt that the three of them were the most powerful of the Dark Guardians. But Connor held my attention like no one else ever had. Whatever the topic was he cared deeply about it. It was evident in his burning expression. I wished he would look at me with that intensity.

"So you wanna go somewhere and talk?" Kayla asked, dragging my attention away from Connor.

My stomach tightened painfully with the thought of any more interrogation. "About what?"

"I don't know. Girl stuff. Wolf stuff. I'm still

adjusting to this whole new lifestyle."

Girl stuff I could handle. Wolf stuff . . . I wasn't so sure I'd be able to talk about it without giving away that I hadn't actually ever experienced it. "I'm going for a humanlike run."

She might invite herself on a four-legged run, but I'd never seen her jog.

She furrowed her delicate brow. "Do you have to work to stay in shape now that you can shift?"

"I love running on two legs. It can't be beat for an adrenaline rush."

Before she had a chance to debunk my statement— since I figured there was truly no greater rush than what one experienced when shifting—I hurried up the stairs to my room, grateful that she didn't follow. I quickly changed into running shorts and sneakers. Grabbing my iPod, I rushed outside before anyone else could stop me and hit the ground running.

As I settled into the familiar rhythm, my mind drifted to Connor. I should have reached over and taken his hand. Squeezed it. Silently communicated that I was there for him. Where was the strong, bold Brittany who had defied the elders and gone off on her own to face the full moon? Yeah, Connor might not be ready for a relationship, but that didn't mean he couldn't use a friend who did more than drool whenever she was in the same room with him.

I shifted my thoughts to Bio-Chrome and our plan to destroy them. Its lead researcher, Dr. Keane, and his son, Mason, wanted to figure out what made Shifters shift. They wanted to replicate it, create some sort of serum that would allow Statics for a short while to have the capabilities of healing and transforming that Shifters did. But in creating their product, they could very likely ruin everything we had. They wanted to capture a Shifter. We had no guarantee that whoever they captured would survive whatever experiments Bio-Chrome had in mind. But worse, they'd reveal our existence to the world. Even if Kayla was correct and it was time to tell humans that Shifters existed, we needed to be able to do it on our terms—not Bio-Chrome's. I wasn't a hundred percent convinced that Statics were ready to accept the existence of Shifters. Bio-Chrome didn't treat us as though we had rights. When they'd captured Lucas, they'd put him in a cage and tormented him.

They would stop at nothing to gain what they wanted—to have our abilities to shift.

I could relate. I'd waited so long for the arrival of the right moon and now that it had passed I was straining to reach the next one—to see if it made a difference.

But Bio-Chrome would kill to gain what they wanted.

SIX

When I returned from my run, Lucas had posted a list-
ing of the teams. Connor had been put in charge of a
team. I wasn't surprised. Lucas depended on him as
much as he depended on Rafe. Connor was good at ana-
lyzing situations. He wasn't afraid of anything. He'd be
a terrific leader. My leader, since I saw my name on the
list below his.

A tiny thrill shot through me. We'd be working together
in close proximity. I just had to hope that whatever we
were assigned to do, we could do it without shifting.

I still had a lot of pent-up energy that needed to be
released, so I headed down to the gym. Some time back,

the basement of Wolford had been converted into a work-out area: two walls of mirrors, two of red brick, and no windows to let in sunlight.

Apparently I wasn't the only one feeling restless. Several guys were lifting weights, including Connor. I received a few nods of acknowledgment, but for the most part my arrival was ignored. I was one of the few girls who'd ever stepped foot in this underground dungeon. Maybe the reason none of the guys had declared me as his mate was because they felt as though I offered competition that none of the other girls did.

I grabbed a towel from the stack by the door and tried to calm my quivering nerves. I'd never been in the gym while Connor was there.

I'd planned to work out with free weights, but the only available bench was beside him, and I just couldn't bring myself to go over there. I headed for the treadmill on the wall perpendicular to the row benches. Connor was no longer in my line of sight. Since I'd just returned from a jog that had left me sweaty, I went straight back into running mode. I turned up the volume on my iPod and got into a rhythm where all my troubles melted away.

A couple of guys stopped to look at me, then returned to what they were doing. As far as I knew, no one gave a flip about an aerobic workout once they were touched by a full moon. After they had the ability to shift, running on all fours was a completely different game. On the brick wall opposite me, someone had slapped a bumper sticker that read, "Real Shifters do it on all fours."

The treadmill was definitely a stupid choice, Brit.

If anyone made a snide comment, I'd claim habit as my excuse. Then I got mad at myself for feeling like I had to justify my actions. I hadn't before. I wasn't going to now. I enjoyed running. So what if I preferred it in biped mode?

I kicked up the tempo and could hear my feet pounding the rubber over Carrie Underwood's voice blasting through my earbuds. She was singing about a guy who wouldn't call, which made me look over at Connor. In one hand, he held a large dumbbell. He curled it up and down with movements so smooth that I almost didn't believe the 40 LBS. stamped on its side. He was wearing shorts and a black T-shirt with the sleeves torn away, leaving ragged edges that made me think he'd used his teeth. It was stupid to find a ratty old T-shirt sexy but I did. He was ripped, of course, like most of the guys were.

I knew he'd been working out for a while because a fine sheen of sweat covered his skin. He still hadn't bothered to shave and his hair looked even more unkempt. He looked rugged and dangerous, a guy accustomed to always winning. Little wonder he wasn't in the happiest of moods since the full moon.

84

Some of the guys were talking to one another, the occasional bark of laughter echoing through the room. But no one talked to him, no one bothered him.

He swung his head in my direction, and I averted my gaze so fast that my eyes nearly bounced around in their sockets. I immediately regretted my reaction. What did I care if he caught me staring at him?

I thought about last night when his gaze had dropped to my lips. I thought about breakfast when I'd caught him studying me, and I remembered the tension between us during the meeting. That electricity had always been one-sided, but now it felt as though it might be flowing both ways.

And just as I had that thought, the fine hairs on my arms raised just a little. I slid my eyes over to Connor. He was looking in the mirror in front of him, but it was obvious that he was looking at me and not himself. He didn't flinch or avert his gaze; his concentration was centered on me. He was still working the weight and his jaw was clenched as though he was straining against something. And I didn't think it was the weight of the dumbbell. It looked like child's play for him.

I wanted to think of something clever to say, something that would indicate that I could take him or leave him—or would indicate my interest if he was interested. I'd never played any of these flirting games. I needed to do a little research, check out some chick flicks with Kate Hudson or Drew Barrymore. But would the torture be worth it? I was more into action flicks.

Before the last full moon, I'd always been honest and upfront with people. Lately I felt as though I wasn't even walking in my own skin anymore.

But I couldn't think of anything to say to Connor. I didn't look away and neither did he. He was slowing his reps and I could see the slightest quiver in his muscles. He probably needed to stop, but he kept going. Watching him straining like that did something to my insides. Suddenly I was fighting to draw in air. I pressed the cool-down button and began slowing my steps to keep up with the machine's preparing to shut down.

I never took my gaze from Connor's. When I finally stopped, I removed my earbuds and stuffed them in my shorts pocket. I wiped the towel over my face, burying it in the soft cotton and mentally preparing myself for what I planned to do.

As deliberately as possible, I walked over to the bench beside Connor, sat, and pulled off my T-shirt, relishing the feel of cool air hitting the damp skin around my sports bra. Watching Connor in the mirror, I thought it looked as though his movements faltered. His eyes narrowed. He started pumping faster. I had this crazy moment of feeling like I was tormenting him, that perhaps he was finally really taking notice of me.

Reaching down, I wrapped a hand around a ten-pound weight. I began mimicking his movements, all the while acutely aware of his gaze wandering over me. I grew warm and languid, the kind of feeling I had when I went to the spa with my mom and spoiled myself with a hot stone massage.

"What are you staring at?" I finally asked.

He shook his head, but didn't look away. "None of the other girls are as devoted to working out as you are."

"I can't help it if they're slackers. I want to be the best Dark Guardian there is, and that means staying in shape."

"Guys will always be better Guardians than girls," someone said.

I jerked my head over to where Drew, a novice, was doing leg squats. It always seemed to me that the novices were a little too cocky when everyone knew that a true Guardian could kick their butts around the moon.

"I could outrun *you*," I said.

"That's stamina not strength."

"So what do you want to do? See who can lift the most weight?"

Grinning, he shook his head. Drew was known for liking to get physical, for inciting fights. I didn't know if the guy was going to make it as a Dark Guardian. He had anger issues he needed to get under control. Around him, a couple of guys stopped what they were doing to pay more attention to us.

"Leave her alone, Drew," Connor said.

"I can fight my own battles," I told him.

He rolled his eyes, demonstrating his impatience with me.

"Isn't that what being a Guardian is about?" I asked.

"It's about fighting with the pack," Connor said.

I knew he was right. It irritated me that he was right. But his order to leave me alone was followed as everyone returned to concentrating on his exercises. When Connor barked, the others usually jumped. I figured if he wasn't good friends with Lucas, if he didn't believe our kind needed to behave with more civility, he might have challenged Lucas for pack leader. I had no doubt he would have won.

In spite of his usual good humor, which had apparently gone into hiding since Lindsey's betrayal, he was one of the toughest Guardians.

So why hadn't he beat Rafe?

"So what's up with you and Daniel?" Connor asked in a low voice.

I almost lost my rhythm. I switched the weight to the other hand while he did the same. "What are you talking about?"

"This morning at breakfast, the way you were acting. Looked like you were reconsidering him for a mate."

"Jealous?" I asked. I realized the moment the words left my mouth that it was the wrong ploy.

"Just curious."

"He's a nice guy, but that's all."

Something shifted between us that I couldn't quite identify. Connor sped up his movements, grunting louder, pumping harder. His eyes were on my reflection in the mirror. I began to move in tandem. The air was thick with heat, as though we were engaged in a contest of wills and weights. The sweat glistened on my skin. I felt a drop roll down the center of my stomach, and watched as Connor's gaze followed it until it reached the waistband of my shorts and was absorbed into the material. His grunts got deeper, harsher. A feral glint lit his eyes. For the first time, in human form, he resembled the ferocious wolf he could transform into. I wasn't sure what was making me more breathless. The way Connor looked or the weight of the dumbbell I was lifting.

Unfortunately, the burn in my arm became too much. As much as I hated to, I had to concede. Panting, I dropped the weight to the floor. Connor kept going. *Be that way.*

Moving away from him, I positioned myself on a nearby mat and began doing stomach crunches. When my arms were rested, no longer quivering, I went to the chin-up bar, jumped, and grabbed onto it, my fingers curling toward me. Facing the brick wall, I brought myself up and back down. All around me, I could hear heavy breathing, the grunting of us working hard, preparing mentally and physically for the battle with Bio-Chrome.

Exerting a great deal of effort, I brought my chin to the very top of the bar before lowering my body again. Over and over, quickening my pace until my arms begged for mercy. I slowed. It was a mistake. Without the momentum, it was too hard. I dropped back to the floor. Bending over, my hands on my thighs, I dragged in deep breaths, relishing the high that came from working out to the max.

"You should always expect an attack," Connor said, his voice low, his warm breath whispering along my neck.

I glared at him over my shoulder. "That's what I'm preparing for."

"You can never be completely prepared."

Before I could respond, he wrapped his arms around me, lifted me up, and slammed me down on the nearby wrestling mat, his body straddling mine. The gym had grown impossibly quiet. How had I not noticed? The only grunts and harsh breathing were coming from Connor and me. The others were circling around to watch the show.

Connor was strong, impossibly strong. I couldn't

match him in strength, but I figured I had agility on my side. With a quick thrust of my leg, I leveraged myself up and slid from beneath him, safely rolling to the side. Part of me wanted to run away. *It's always the smartest choice.*

But another part, the part that had desperately longed for the moment when I would be able to shift, commanded me to pounce.

I jumped onto Connor's back, wrapping my arms around his chest. Instincts drove me to sweep my left leg against his knee, causing him to lose his balance. As we fell, he turned just in time, putting me on bottom. But it didn't matter, I was in control and he knew it.

Connor's body flexed, his muscles knotting up, and with one slick move he was again in charge. For several minutes we changed positions. Never speaking, bodies sliding over each other's. At times, it was difficult to tell where my skin ended and his began. Connor's body was slick from working out, making it hard to grab on to. But so was mine. His hands, large and powerful, slid down my back and across my thighs. My fingers were digging into his shoulders.

We broke apart and scrambled to our feet. Breathing heavily, we circled each other. His eyes held the glint of a predator, along with something more. I could feel the tension in the air—but it had nothing to do with competitors.

It was all about girl-boy. The sexual awareness was humming between us.

"You're good," Connor said, and I heard the respect in his voice.

I wanted to swell up with pride, but I didn't dare let my defenses down.

"I told you she would be." It was Lucas. I hadn't seen him come into the room. I wondered how long he'd been observing.

Connor gave a barely perceptible nod and then he was coming for me again. He went high and I went low, grabbing his leg and using his own weight to toss him to the floor. In the fierce moments that followed, I twisted around, grabbed his arm, slammed his elbow across my thigh, and torqued it. Some referred to the maneuver as an arm lock, but I seldom paid attention to the technicalities. I just knew it gave me an advantage when my opponent was bigger than I was. Connor roared, the beast within him not at all happy with being restrained.

I felt his muscles relaxing, knew he was about to surrender. I loosened my grip—

He had me on the floor, his body pressing down on mine before I could blink. I stared up into his blue eyes. Maybe he thought he had me where he wanted me, but the truth was that I had him exactly where I'd always wanted him—so close, skin on skin.

I watched as his gaze wandered over me as though he was trying to figure out exactly who I was. His head dropped just a fraction, his nostrils flared, and I knew he was inhaling my scent. I had an urge to say something stupid, like, "Let's make love, not war." It would be just like me to ruin an intense moment with a cheesy one-liner.

But luckily my survival instincts were on high alert, controlling the part of my brain associated with speech. Instead, I just said, "I'm done here."

Connor's heated gaze settled on my mouth with more intensity than it had last night. Then it shifted up to my eyes. His brow furrowed. Finally, he nodded and rolled off me. He held his hand out to me and I wrapped mine around it, feeling the strength of his hold and roughness of his palm. Both sent pleasure rippling through me as he pulled me to my feet.

"Okay," Connor said, looking past me. "She'll do."

"What?" I jerked my head around to see Lucas, arms crossed over his chest, appearing incredibly pleased with himself. Beside him, Kayla smiled at me.

"Connor's in charge of his own group of Guardians," Lucas said.

"Yeah, I saw the list on the wall," I told him.

"Every leader needs a second in command he trusts to guard his back," Lucas said. "I suggested Connor select you, but he had his doubts. Think you just beat those into the ground."

I glared at Connor. He was running a towel over his slick skin as though he had no idea of the magnitude of what I'd felt pinned to the floor beneath him: the way my heart had pumped with more force than it ever had, how I'd thought he was actually becoming more interested in me as . . . a girl. I swung back and slammed my fist into his arm.

"Hey!" He rubbed his arm. "What the hell?"

"You were *testing* me? Testing *me*? God, Connor, you've known me forever, and you had doubts about me?"

Anger burned in his eyes, but I had a feeling it didn't come close to what he was seeing in mine. "Sorry if you're offended, but I've never seen you in warrior mode, so yeah, I wanted to confirm what you're capable of."

I got right up in his face. "Don't you *dare* try to test me in wolf form. If you do, you won't be getting up from the mat." It was a lie, bravado that I couldn't back up with action, but I didn't care. I wasn't going to let anyone force me into revealing my dirty little secret.

The challenge darkened his expression, turned his anger into something primal—and my body reacted strongly to the message he was sending. Suddenly we were breathing heavily as though we were near the end of a workout, our hands tightened into fists—not to fight but to control the impulse to touch. It took every bit of willpower I possessed not to pounce and take us both to floor. I could tell he was engaged in the same battle. He was scenting me again, and I was afraid my fragrance was laced with the heat of passion.

"Oookay," Lucas said, putting his arm against Connor's chest and pushing him back. "We get it. No more tests."

The awareness between us broke. I felt like I was coming out of a trance.

"I mean it," I snarled, before storming through the room. Shifters moved out of my way as though I were made of silver.

In the hallway, I heard the patter of rapid footsteps.

"Brittany, wait up," Kayla said.

I spun around so fast that she staggered back. I could only imagine what my expression was showing: the hurt, the anger, the disappointment.

"I take it you knew about this . . . test or whatever the hell it was."

She looked startled by my vehemence, but as far as I knew no other Guardian had ever been *tested*. Why me? Did they sense that the moon had betrayed me? Were they afraid I'd do the same to them?

Kayla appeared uncomfortable. "In a way. I knew if Connor saw a chance to assess your skills, he was going to take it."

"And you didn't think to give me a heads-up?"

"I tried," she said flatly. "But you wanted to go running."

Damn. She had tried. Now I felt bad for taking my frustration out on her. She was new to our society. She hadn't grown up in it. She didn't understand the subtleties, didn't know everything we were capable of. The fury seeped out of me. "The girl stuff, the wolf stuff? You couldn't have been a little less cryptic?"

"I didn't want anyone to overhear us and know that I was going against orders. Everyone around here has such incredibly sensitive hearing. I don't know how anyone keeps a secret."

I shook my head, the fear of discovery spiking. "They don't usually." Now it was my turn to feel uncomfortable. "I'm sorry. I shouldn't have taken my anger at Connor out on you."

"It doesn't matter. I'd have been pissed, too. But, hey, you handled yourself better than anyone else would have."

The results of the test finally slammed home. I'd passed. Connor was giving me a position of great responsibility. I'd impressed him—but for how long? Until the first time that he needed me to shift. And when I couldn't, all the respect I'd worked so hard to attain would dissolve. I considered going back in the gym and telling him the truth, but I was tough. I'd just proven it. I could be a valuable asset—as long as a situation didn't arrive where we had to shift. I didn't want to lose this opportunity to be with Connor, so I pretended everything was okay, that my nerves weren't suddenly jangling. I grinned. "I kicked his butt."

"Almost . . . Until the end anyway."

I didn't respond. What could I say to that? Deny what everyone had seen?

"Don't let it get you down," Kayla said. "You put up a good fight. You should hang with Lucas and me tonight."

"Yeah, getting scorched while you two get it on sounds like fun."

She gave me an indulgent smile. "We'll behave. Lucas told me about the media room—that it has a huge flat screen hooked into a DVD player. A bunch of us are going to watch movies tonight. I'm hoping for something with Brad Pitt."

"Good luck with that. These guys tend to go with the worst movies ever made."

She shrugged, being a good sport about it. "That works, too. The main thing is to be part of the pack."

And no doubt making out while the lights were low.

The door to the dungeon opened, and Connor strode out. He nodded in acknowledgment as he went past me.

Tremors cascaded through me. I was used to them

happening after a hard workout, but I knew these had nothing to do with my exhausted muscles. They were all because of Connor.

I'd seen him fight in wolf form when we encountered an animal in the wild that threatened us. I'd thought he looked beautiful, but lethal. But I'd never seen him in warrior mode as a human. He was as sexy as hell and even more dangerous.

Especially because I saw in his eyes that he knew the truth about what I'd done. I'd let him win.

SEVEN

The long hot shower I took back in our room made my body go wonderfully languid. But it tensed right back up when I was toweling off and spotted bruises forming on my thigh and upper arm. In frustration I hit my balled fist on the counter. Any self-respecting Shifter would shift and heal those suckers right up. My solution was going to be carefully selecting clothes that didn't show too much skin.

That's so not going to get Connor's attention.

I couldn't believe that in less than an hour, after his ridiculous test, I caught myself looking forward to seeing him again. I couldn't deny that wrestling him had been a total turn-on—even if the reason for it had sucked.

After our close encounter on the wrestling mat, I knew I'd finally caught his undivided attention and that result was more invigorating than being given a position of authority. He'd scented the pheromones my body had been releasing with his nearness. I wondered what might have happened if we hadn't had an audience in the dungeon. Would he have dipped his head farther for a kiss? Would he have objected if I'd slipped my hands beneath his shirt and caressed the firm muscles of his back? Would he have pressed—

A hard thud on the bathroom door made my heart leap into my throat.

"Hey, Brittany, can I come in?" Lindsey asked.

When did she get back to the room? And couldn't she have waited until I was finished with my fantasy to disturb me? "I'm not dressed," I ground out.

"So wrap up in a towel. I need to get ready for Rafe."

"Give me a minute." I didn't bother to hide my irritation. And I couldn't afford to take time to see where my fantasy might have led. Maybe tonight before I went to sleep. I gave my body a quick once-over and didn't see any other bruising.

I wrapped a towel around my torso, but the bruise on my thigh peeked out like a naughty kid I'd once babysat.

Great. Maybe Kayla wouldn't notice. Lindsey knew the truth, so my injuries wouldn't come as a surprise to her. I grabbed another towel and walked out rubbing it over my arm like I was drying it for the first time—hoping to keep the bruise hidden.

"Thanks," Lindsey said as she scooted past me and closed the door.

Kayla was zipping up a short jean skirt when I tossed the towel on the bed and started scrounging through my backpack. My bruised arm was hidden from her view. I dug out a pair of jeans. As for the shirt—

"Is that a bruise?" Kayla asked.

Looking down at my thigh, I feigned surprise. "Huh. Looks like."

"So shift and heal it." She pulled a lacy green top over her head. "That's one of the coolest things about being a Shifter. How easily we heal."

She grabbed a brush and started dragging it through her vibrant red hair.

"I'll take care of it after you guys leave." But not in the way she thought.

She stilled the brush. "I'll close my eyes if you're modest about shifting in front of me."

"Thanks, but I'll deal with it."

"I understand," she said quietly.

I doubt it. "Understand what?"

"It's a personal experience. The first time I shifted in front of someone other than Lucas, I was so nervous I wasn't certain I could pull it off. I can't imagine what it must have been like growing up knowing you'd have this amazing ability. I don't know that I would have had the patience to wait."

"It's not like we have a choice."

"True." She put her brush aside, headed for the door, and stopped. "Sure you don't want me to wait for you?"

"I'm sure. Besides, you and Lucas can probably get in a hundred kisses before I'm finished getting ready."

"Or one long, slow one. My personal favorite." Opening the door, she smiled brightly. "Hey!"

"Hey," Lucas said, his voice reflecting how glad he was to see her.

She closed the door. How great it would be to have a guy waiting for me in the hallway. But only if that guy was Connor.

I dressed quickly, before Lindsey came out of the bathroom. I didn't need more advice on how to handle my bruises, and I figured her solution would involve lecturing me that it was confession time.

I tossed my head around and let my hair go free. I imagined Connor combing his fingers through it, over and over until it dried.

I needed to stop thinking about him and get a life.

Maybe the elders were right. Maybe my true soul mate resided in another state, another country even.

Okay, so I hadn't shifted yet, and things were a little different for me but that didn't mean that I didn't deserve a soul mate—or at least a boyfriend. I didn't need a lifetime commitment. But a kiss would be nice. Connor's tongue sliding over mine—

I sighed deeply. I didn't know if I could be happy with anyone who wasn't Connor. Could he be happy with someone who wasn't Lindsey?

The bathroom door clicked open and she strode out, looking great as always. She was supermodel slender. I'd never been that thin. My grandfather had once told me that I had good bone structure. *Yeah, that's the kind of compliment every girl longs for.*

"I heard that you're teaming up with Connor," Lindsey said, as she flung her bundle of dirty clothes into a corner near her bed.

"It's not like it's a secret. It's posted on the wall outside the council room."

"I want things to work out for you two, I really do. But Connor seemed . . . a little distant today."

"Well, duh? You kinda made a fool of him, Linds. Something I'd never do."

A deep red blush stained her cheeks. "I should have been as strong as you sooner—when I realized Rafe was the one. I just didn't want to hurt Connor. I mean, everyone thought we belonged together. Only we didn't."

I didn't respond. There was nothing I could say to make her feel better. She left quietly, and I sat on my bed wondering how I should spend the evening. The girls I usually hung around with—Kayla and Lindsey—would be busy getting hot and heavy with their mates. Which left the only member of our team not tied to someone— Connor. But as much as I wanted to see him, my irritation with him was returning, and I wasn't in the mood to chase him. I was starting to feel that sting of disappointment that he didn't know me well enough to know I'd work my butt off to be the best Dark Guardian.

Tonight I was on my own.

After scooping up a tub of warm popcorn from the machine in the hallway and lacing it generously with butter, I slipped inside the media room that closely resembled a tiny theater. The lights were already out, the movie in progress. I almost reached for a small penlight that I usually carried in a pocket, before I remembered that I was now *supposed* to have great vision in the dark.

With the Guardians, several novices, house staff, and the elders here, almost every seat was taken. And of course, as fate would have it, at that precise moment our hero was staggering through a dark forest trying to outrun the full moon. Yeah, werewolf movies were on the top of our must-watch list. Hollywood's take on our kind was hilariously off-base. It became more difficult to locate an empty chair. I heard the door open and close too quickly to give me enough light to see.

Then someone touched my arm and a jolt of pleasure rippled through me, and the earlier irritation I'd felt toward Connor dissipated. Even in the near-darkness without a clear vision of him, I knew it was Connor. I recognized his scent.

"Waiting for someone?" Connor whispered near my ear, sending delicious shivers over my neck.

Only you, corny as it was, popped into my mind. "Uh, no."

"Then sit with me."

Before I could respond, Connor wrapped his hand around mine and our fingers intertwined. My heart skipped a little bit at how much longer and stronger his fingers were than mine. I'd felt them running over my body while we'd wrestled, but for some reason this moment seemed much more intimate. Connor was a few inches taller than me and a little broader—and I remembered how that body had pressed down on me earlier.

The scene on the screen suddenly brightened as it focused on the full moon, and I could see a little more clearly. Connor led me toward seats in front of Kayla and

Lucas. Kayla had never had much of a poker face. Her eyes widened with surprise that I didn't think had anything to do with the movie.

I fought not to feel the loss as Connor released his hold on my hand. Sitting down, I got comfortable before offering him some popcorn. Grinning, he took a handful before settling back to watch the movie, our close encounter this afternoon apparently forgotten.

I wasn't sure exactly what I'd been expecting. His arm coming around me, his lips pressing against mine. I munched on popcorn that tasted like sawdust—not its fault. I'd just lost my appetite.

The guy in the movie was suddenly sprouting hair in little weird tufts on his face and hands. Bad special effects began lengthening his snout. I had a feeling this movie had gone straight to video.

"Give me a break," Connor muttered and started tossing popcorn at the screen. He wasn't the only one. Boos and hisses echoed around us.

"Who found this one?" Lucas called out.

"Daniel!" someone yelled.

"It's definitely in the running."

There was an unspoken competition to find the worst werewolf movie ever made. We had an unusual sense of what qualified as entertainment. Usually I laughed along with everyone else and made fun of what we all considered a parody of our kind. But tonight, watching a transformation—even one that was so far removed from reality as to be comical—hit just a little too close to home.

For as long as I could remember I'd defined myself as what I would become when I turned seventeen and faced my first full moon. All the insecurities that I'd felt because no guy had ever paid any attention to me would have melted away. In wolf form, I would have possessed beauty, confidence, and power. I'd never have to worry that some guy would abandon me the way my father had abandoned my mother and me.

I was suddenly very much aware of Connor's arm on the back of my chair, his knuckles feathering along my cheek. The contact was such a surprise my whole body stiffened.

"Hey, what's wrong?" His voice was low and deep, his mouth so near my ear that I could easily hear him in spite of the catcalls and whistles as the werewolf on the screen completed his transformation—without ever removing his clothes. Neat trick.

I shook my head. "Nothing."

He slid his hand around the back of my neck and began stroking the underside of my chin with his thumb. Heat pooled in my stomach. I was acutely aware of him studying me, while I tried to give the impression my attention was locked on the screen. I'd had so many dreams about moments like this with Connor, but now that one had arrived I didn't quite trust it. A few nights ago, he'd been prepared to commit his life, his heart, his body, his soul to Lindsey forever. Now he was giving attention to me as though she'd never existed, as though he hadn't had a symbol of her name inked onto his skin in an ancient ritual that was supposed to identify them as mates. And he'd felt a need to test me. Maybe I'd just test him back.

His lips touched my ear and my resolve to be tough where he was concerned shattered. I exhaled in a jagged breath. I thought I was going to melt into the seat. "Let's go," he ordered.

Before I could object—not that I would have—he stood, grabbed my hand, pulled me to my feet, and led me out of the media room. In the hallway, he faced me. "Something *is* wrong. I know you're not still mad about this afternoon or you wouldn't have sat with me. Something else is bothering you. What is it?"

His voice emanated power and command. I wanted to tell him the truth. I wanted him to reassure me that somewhere I would find an answer, that I would become the beautiful wolf I'd always longed to be. But I remembered the odd looks I'd received when I'd hopped onto the treadmill. Those looks were nothing compared with the ones I'd get if the truth about me came out.

"It's this Bio-Chrome mess." Partly true. "I just

wasn't in the mood to watch a movie making fun of what we are. Mason and his dad view us as little more than lab rats to be dissected and studied, and portrayals like that"—I jerked my head toward the theater—"don't help our cause. We're stereotyped."

"No, we're not, Brittany. No one knows we exist. Well, except for Bio-Chrome. The movies are fiction, based on someone's imagination or fears. We know they're grossly inaccurate but we can't be accurately portrayed if we're not willing to come out of the woods."

His words surprised me. "Do you think we should?" I asked.

"Some of us have been talking about it, but you heard the elders. They believe there's safety in secrecy."

"Is that what you believe?"

"I'd rather face the storm." He reached into the tub of popcorn and grabbed a handful. "Let's get out of here."

"Like where?"

"Just walk."

He took the tub I still clutched and tossed it into a nearby trash can. Wrapping his hand around mine, he led me outside. Usually I wasn't so docile, but tonight wherever he led was where I wanted to go.

We reached the edge of the yard, where it gave way to the woods. Leaning against a tree, Connor put his hands on my hips and brought me in alignment with him. My heart thundering, our eyes met and held. Very slowly, he skimmed his hand down my arm, and I hated that I'd had to wear sleeves to hide the bruise, that I couldn't feel the rasp of his touch over my skin. He threaded his fingers through mine, and a spark of electricity shot between us. Then he lifted my hand and began to lick any lingering butter and salt off my fingertips. It was probably the most sensual thing I'd ever experienced. But it didn't feel . . . I don't know. Honest.

"I won't be your rebound girl," I said, pushing the words up out of my throat.

He seemed surprised by my harsh tone. "Lindsey told me that you have the hots for me."

I slid my eyes closed and groaned. She had no right. I opened my eyes to find him still studying me.

"Well?" he prodded.

I gritted my teeth, hoping he wasn't about to make a fool of me. But this was Connor. The Connor who'd gone to school with me. The one on the football field who I rooted for. The one who carried campers' equipment into the wilderness and never complained. The one with the sexy smile. The one who—if I was honest—cared enough about our kind to make sure he was choosing the right person to serve as his right hand. "Yeah, so?"

"How much?"

"It's not something I can quantify on a scale of one

to ten." Mostly because what I felt for him was off the charts.

"Was it like you just looked at me one day and *bam!*— you were struck by lightning?"

"No."

"That's the way Lucas said it was with Kayla. That when you meet your destined mate it's like taking a kick to the gut."

"Well, that's romantic," I said sarcastically. "Why does it have to be like that? Why can't we just gradually fall in love? The way humans do."

"Because we're not human." He pulled me closer until my hips rammed against his. "You let me win this afternoon. You relaxed your hold before I indicated that I was giving up. You know better than to do that."

What I'd misread for desire, I now realized bordered on anger, maybe disappointment that I'd let him win. I swallowed hard. "I figured your ego took a pounding when Rafe beat you. I couldn't do that to you again—not in front of the others."

"You think Rafe beat me?" he asked, slowly enunciating each word as though he found them difficult to comprehend.

"Well, yeah, I know how these things work. A challenge is always a fight to the death, and neither of you died, but Rafe ended up with the girl, which means he won but showed mercy." I realized how awful that sounded, and that I was babbling. So untypical, but I wanted desperately to explain why I'd thrown the fight. "Believe me, if I'd been betting money, I would have bet on you. You're not as in-your-face as Lucas is or as intimidating as Rafe, but you're powerful and strong and I think you're the best of—"

"Just shut up," he growled, right before he covered my mouth with his.

I felt as though I'd waited my whole life for this moment—to kiss Connor. And it was just as feverish and wild as I'd expected. How could it not be when one of us was fortunate enough to harbor a beast inside of him?

My mind stuttered with the reminder that my beast had yet to be released, but I shoved it aside to concentrate on the kiss. My skin tingled where the stubble on his chin abraded mine. There was hunger in his kiss, heated passion, and unexpected tenderness. His strong hands roamed over my back, slipped beneath my shirt, and skimmed across my spine into the curve of my lower back. I moaned softly. I wanted his shirt off. I wanted my fingers trailing over his chest. His hands clamped my hips, and suddenly he was pushing me away.

"He didn't beat me," he ground out. "I walked away because I didn't love Lindsey."

"But—"

"Yeah, I know. Ink on my shoulder. Public declaration she's the one. Well, she wasn't. You don't want to be the rebound girl? Fine, but don't tease me with that fine-honed body either."

Before I could respond, he started to run, discarding his clothes as he went. As he disappeared into the thicket of trees, he transformed into the wolf, the moonlight dancing over his golden fur in the same way that my fingers ached to.

Was he expecting me to strip down, transform, and follow? Was that how I was supposed to prove that I hadn't been teasing him earlier, that I wanted more than kisses from him? By chasing after him?

Breathing heavily, I turned around and placed my back against the tree. What had just happened? Had the test in the gym come about not because Connor had seen it as an ideal opportunity to test my skills, but because . . . well, because he'd been attracted to me? He'd wanted to get up close and personal—and challenging me had provided him with an acceptable excuse?

He didn't love Lindsey. The words kept echoing over and over in my mind, like a song that I couldn't get out of my head. If he hadn't loved her, there was no rebound. And if there was no rebound—

Was it possible that I could have Connor on my terms?

Yes, right up until the moment when he realized I'd yet to turn into a wolf, that I'd couldn't lope along beside him. That he could hint that I should follow but I still wasn't able to catch up. That, for now, I was only half of what he was.

There was none of the magic that bonded two mates forever. No sharing of moonlight.

I couldn't go on like this. I didn't want to confess it to the elders, but my mom—I could tell her. She'd be back from Europe tomorrow. She might know what was going on. Maybe she was a late bloomer as well.

Dejected by my present reality, I began walking back to the residence. I decided to use the approved front door for my entrance this time. As I rounded the corner, I nearly ran into a couple locked in a passionate embrace. His back was up against the brick and she was up against him. As they kissed, he moaned and she sighed. They reminded me of what I'd just left.

Although I hadn't made any noise, they both suddenly broke apart. Lindsey released a startled laugh. "Oh my God, I thought I smelled Connor."

Without a word, I started walking on. She grabbed my arm and spun me around. "I do smell him," she said. "You've been with him . . . like, right up against him."

I was beginning to hate how much they could pick up from scent. Nothing was sacred around here.

"So?" I snapped. "You ditched him. What I do with him is none of your business."

"No. I know. I mean, I think it's great. I want him to move on. I just didn't think it would happen so fast."

"Yeah, well, it's a mixed review."

"What do you mean?"

Rafe came up behind her and slid his arms around her waist and rested his chin on the top of her head. They fit together like perfect pieces for an "Over the Moon" puzzle. Did they have to constantly touch? Could they even begin to understand that as happy as I was for them, it still hurt to see them having what I didn't?

I glared at Rafe, hoping to at least get him to back off a few feet. I wasn't going to discuss Connor with Lindsey while he hovered. Hell, I hadn't even made up my mind if I was going to tell her anything.

She lifted a shoulder. "You can go ahead and talk in front of him. He can read my mind."

"Only when he's in wolf form."

"No, actually, pretty much anytime," Rafe said.

I stared at Lindsey. "Anytime . . . anything?"

"Yeah, but he's bound by my oaths to keep secrets."

Great. Absolutely great. Eventually everyone would know.

"So what happened with Connor?" Lindsey prodded.

I made a shooing motion. "I don't care if he can read

your mind. I can't talk with him looking at me."

I'd expected Lindsey to stay stubborn, so I could be equally stubborn and walk away. Instead she twisted around, reached up, and kissed Rafe on the cheek. "I'll find you."

No doubt with that amazing nose she now possessed. Without a word, Rafe spun on his heel and strode away. Lindsey faced me and waited, while I tried to determine how much to tell her.

"Come on," she finally said and took my hand, leading me over to the massive stone steps that led up to the door. Snarling stone wolves sat on pedestals on either side of them. I didn't know why all the wolves around here had to be snarling. I guessed they were symbolic, indicating we wouldn't take crap from anyone.

Lindsey and I dropped down to the steps. They were hard beneath my butt, which was a good thing because it ensured we wouldn't get comfy and talk too long.

"So . . . he kissed you?" she asked hesitantly.

"It was"—I sighed deeply with the memory—"amazing while it lasted. Then Connor ran off. He thinks I've been teasing him. Why did you tell him I had the hots for him?"

She appeared embarrassed. "Maybe I was trying to make up for what happened during the full moon. It was awful, Brit. I didn't want to hurt him like that, and I thought if he knew someone else liked him that he might feel better."

I debated how much to reveal. I didn't want to hurt her either, but—

"He told me that he didn't love you."

With her hands pressed between her knees, she leaned forward. "Yeah, he told me the same thing. I thought maybe he was just saying it. You know how much pride these guys have." She looked back over her shoulder at me. "You think he meant it?"

I did, but whatever the relationship between them was then and now was between them. "I don't know." I tapped her arm with my knuckles. "Hey, thanks for not outing me during the meeting this morning."

"I promised to keep your secret, but sooner or later . . . it can put us in danger."

Talk about trying to be politically correct. I knew she'd wanted to say I—*me*—would put us in danger. I also knew that I was putting the *others* at risk. Was I being totally selfish?

"My mom comes back tomorrow. Maybe you're right. Maybe my birth certificate is wrong. Could be a year off or something. I'll talk to her."

"They won't kick you out of the pack if you're . . . different," she assured me.

"But I can't be a Dark Guardian."

"It limits you if you can't shift," she admitted.

"Yeah, I know. I can't smell who's been making out with whom."

She playfully nudged her shoulder against mine, as though she understood that I was struggling to make light of this dire situation. "It's more than that."

"I know," I said, all teasing aside. "If my mom doesn't have any answers, if during the next full moon nothing happens . . . I'll out myself. Leave the society."

"I don't think you have to go that far. There's bound to be something you can do. Man the computers or something."

"Lindsey, I've been preparing my entire life to be a warrior. I never wanted anything as much as I wanted to be a wolf. It's so hard to be here right now. Tonight when Connor shifted, I had this sense of wonder that he had the ability to transform into this glorious creature and at the same time I felt an overwhelming loss because I hadn't yet experienced that. I'm tired of being just plain, dull Brittany." I stopped there before I confessed that I understood where Bio-Chrome was coming from. They had to be like me, envying what they were not capable of achieving.

I could tell that Lindsey was at a loss for words. What reassurances could she offer? Neither of us knew what was going on with me. I shoved myself to my feet. "Good night."

When I got to my room it was empty. I figured Kayla was either still watching the werewolf marathon or she and Lucas had sneaked out for a little personal time like Lindsey and Rafe had. My money was on the sneaking out. Ah, young love. Gag.

But I wanted it, too.

After getting ready for bed, I stared at the moonlight coming in through the window and studied the patterns it made on my legs. The full moon was gone, heading toward a new moon, a dark moon.

I tried to imagine my skin tingling with the touch of the moonlight, the way it had tingled when Connor had touched it with his fingertips. His fingers were rough and callused from all the outdoor activity he engaged in, but they'd whispered across my back. I grew warm thinking about it, almost as warm as I'd grown when it had been happening. I tried to push him out of my mind.

But when I fell asleep, as usual, he was there waiting for me in my dreams.

EIGHT

The next morning when I went down to breakfast, I saw
no sign of Connor. Since I wasn't in a social mood, I took
an empty table in the corner. I attacked my breakfast with
a vengeance, so absorbed in it that I didn't notice Lucas
until he was sitting beside me.

With an arched brow, my only acknowledgment of
his presence, I drank down my black coffee, knowing I
was going to have to have a session with teeth whitener
soon. He seemed amused by my attitude.

But when I set down my cup, he grew deadly serious.
"We need to talk."

I shrugged. "So talk."

"Here probably isn't the best place."

I glanced around. Some people were blatantly staring, the polite ones tried to hide their interest. I was probably just getting paranoid, but I felt as though they were all viewing me as the freak I was.

"So where?" I asked, working not to let my discomfort make its way into my voice.

We went to the rooftop. It was strangely liberating up there. When I looked out, all I could see was forest stretching toward the horizon and distant mountains.

"Whenever I forget what it is we're supposed to protect I come up here," Lucas said with reverence. "I think about the summer solstice when our kind gathers here to celebrate our existence. I think about how fragile it is. How much we could lose if our existence becomes known."

So he shared the same concerns as the elders. Not surprising since one was his grandfather.

"Like Kayla, Connor thinks maybe we should reveal our existence," I told him.

He smiled. "Yeah, I know. Maybe they're right. But if they're not, it's not something we'd be able to undo."

The dilemma was similar to the struggle I was facing about whether I should talk with the elders. But without knowing exactly how they'd react, I'd be taking a chance of being relieved of my position as a Dark Guardian. Once I announced that I hadn't shifted, I wouldn't be able to undo it.

I sat on the edge of the short brick wall. "So is that what you wanted to talk to me about—convincing Connor that we need to remain a secret?"

His smile broadened. "No. I doubt Connor's beliefs can be changed, but I also trust him not to betray us like my brother did." His older brother, Devlin, had told Mason that Shifters existed. Lucas grew serious. "Connor and I talked up here last night. We agreed that I needed to make some adjustments with the teams. I've transferred you to mine."

Slowly I pushed myself off the wall. "What? But I passed that stupid test."

"It's got nothing to do with the test." He furrowed his brow. "Well, maybe it does. Connor thinks it's too distracting having you on his team. I agree."

I swore harshly. "I don't understand. Is this because I wouldn't follow him into the woods?"

He looked taken aback. "I don't know anything about that."

"I'll talk to him, convince him—"

"He and his team left late last night."

I sat back down, welcoming the discomfort of the brick cutting into my legs. I didn't understand. I should have told Connor that I hadn't been teasing him, that I'd realized I wasn't a replacement for Lindsey. If we just had a little more time together, to get to know each other—

"I've assigned Rafe his own team. You'll replace him as my second in command," Lucas continued.

I peered up at him. "Like a consolation prize?"

"It's not like that. You've always been more devoted than anyone in preparing to become a Guardian. You'll be an asset to me."

Any other time I would have been thrilled with our pack leader's assessment of me. But right now, all I could think about was Connor and how I could make things right between us.

"So where did Connor's team go?"

"Back to Tarrant, prowling along the way."

Prowling. Which meant they were traveling in wolf form. Maybe being kicked off Connor's team wasn't such a bad thing.

"They'll probably be at the Sly Fox tonight." The Sly Fox was the local hangout. Bad food and music, but a great atmosphere. "Then I'm sending them on to the lab, to observe it while we prepare."

I nodded. Maybe I'd get a chance to see Connor tonight, to figure out exactly where I stood with him. If nowhere, I needed to know that. If something between us was possible, I needed to know that, too.

"You're taking this better than I thought you would," Lucas said.

"You took a chance bringing me up here. I might have decided to fling myself off the roof."

He laughed. "Not you. If anything, I was worried you'd toss me off."

I smiled at that. I guessed I *did* have a reputation for being tough. "So what now?"

"I'm going to meet with the guy who can give us some tips on how to bring down the Bio-Chrome lab without creating a fire hazard. Then Kayla and I are driving back to Tarrant. I've got the patrollers' backpacks I need to drop off at the entrance to the national park. Other things that need transporting. But there's room in my jeep if you want to ride with us. Or you can make your own way back."

As a hiker—my only option—it would take too long, longer by far than as a wolf. Wolves could attain a burst of speed up to forty miles an hour, but they couldn't maintain it for long. Not even Shifters. In wolf form, it would take longer to reach the park entrance than by car. So it would be perfectly reasonable for me to accept the reprieve he offered. "I'd rather go with you. I think my mom is supposed to be back from her trip today. I'm anxious to see her."

I wondered how many lies and excuses I could get away with before Lucas became suspicious. He wasn't stupid.

*   *   *

I started to regret that I hadn't decided to just hike it on my own when I climbed into the back of the jeep behind Lucas and Kayla. It was like I had a front row seat to just-discovered love as they smiled at each other and held hands as much as possible during the journey. I didn't resent that they had each other, but seeing them together was a constant reminder of what I didn't have. I spent a lot of time staring out the window, watching the scenery rush by.

At one point, I asked, "So how did your meeting with the imploding guy go?"

Lucas met my gaze in the rearview mirror. "He offered a lot of suggestions. I don't know if that's the way we'll go though. He needs plans of the building. If it's a secret facility, we may not be able to find anything in the public records."

"What are you going to do then?"

"Do some research. Maybe send in a spy. I don't know. I'm going to talk with my dad."

His dad had once been the leader of the Dark Guardians. Then he'd handed the position over to his older son, who had betrayed us by revealing our existence to Bio-Chrome. I figured Lucas felt as though he had something to prove, to show everyone that he was nothing like his brother.

Kayla looked back over her shoulder at me. "So last night. At the movie. You and Connor."

"It wasn't like it was a date. We just both got there at the same time." I shrugged as though it wasn't a big deal. "So we sat together."

"And you left together."

I sighed. "Are you hinting at something?"

"Just wondering how you feel about him."

"You know, I really don't know." I wasn't about to confess how much I cared for him, not with Lucas there. So many things in my life weren't working out exactly as I'd planned. I was trying to limit collateral damage, how many things people would want to give me sympathy for.

"Well, I think you're cute together," Kayla said.

Ringing endorsement.

"I'll keep that in mind," I said with a grin.

Then Kayla turned her attention back to Lucas, and I shifted my gaze back to the passing scenery. It was the middle of summer, and the foliage was thick. Sunlight dappled through the trees, creating a mosaic of brightness and shadows. It was all so beautiful.

Then something—a dark furry mound?—came into my line of vision too quickly for me to be sure.

"Wait! Lucas, stop!" I yelled.

"What is it?" he asked.

"Just stop. I saw something back there."

Before the jeep came to a complete shuddering stop, I was out the door and racing back in the direction from where we'd come. I leaped over a narrow ravine. Dried leaves and twigs crunched beneath my boots as I searched frantically for what I'd seen. Exactly where had it been?

And then I saw it, and my heart leaped into my throat. I staggered to a halt and knelt beside the fallen wolf. It was unnaturally still, its chest barely rising with each shallow breath.

"What's wrong with it? Is it dying?" Kayla asked as she and Lucas crouched beside me.

"I don't know," I whispered. I stroked it tenderly, my fingers combing through the black fur until they encountered something hard. Gingerly, I parted the fur.

"A tranquilizer dart," Lucas said angrily, reaching for it and tugging it out. Dropping his head back, he inhaled deeply. "Bio-Chrome. I smell Mason. The guy reeks."

Slowly we all glanced around. I couldn't smell them, but I could definitely detect a disharmony in the forest.

"Why would they do this?" Kayla asked.

"Maybe they thought it was a Shifter," I responded.

"But why leave it?" she asked.

I didn't have an answer for that. Neither did Lucas.

"They could still be around," Kayla said.

Lucas shook his head. "The scent isn't strong enough."

"I feel like I still have so much to learn," Kayla said.

Lucas took her hand. "You're doing fine. This Bio-Chrome stuff—it's not what we usually have to worry about."

"What are we going to do about the wolf?" I asked. "We can't leave it like this, vulnerable to predators."

"I'll shift and stay with it," Lucas said. "Then I want to do some reconnaissance. See what else I can pick up. You go back to the jeep, drive into town, and I'll meet you at the Sly Fox tonight."

"I don't want to leave you alone," Kayla said.

"I'll be fine," Lucas assured her.

If I could have shifted, I'd have volunteered to stay behind. Instead, I got to my feet. I needed to leave so Lucas could shift. I also wanted them to have a couple of minutes alone to say good-bye. "I'll meet you back at the jeep. Be careful," I said.

Lucas grinned. "Will do."

I took a step and heard something crack beneath my hiking boot. Bending down, I picked up a broken microscope slide smeared with blood. "Okay, this is something we don't see in the forest every day."

I showed it to Lucas and Kayla.

"Huh," Lucas said. "They must be traveling with some kind of lab equipment so they can test blood. That's the reason they left the wolf. They were able to figure out it was pure wolf."

"Then they leave it behind, vulnerable." I couldn't stop the anger from resonating through me. It was one thing to come after Shifters, but now they were putting innocent wolves in danger.

The wolf began to slowly stir.

"He's not going to be happy when he's fully awake," Lucas said. "You need to go."

"Like I said, be careful," I reminded him before I headed back.

A couple of minutes later, Kayla joined me at the jeep, Lucas's clothes bundled in her arms.

"I can't believe I thought Mason was a nice guy," she said.

"I thought he was, too," I told her. "He's just gotten obsessed."

She got behind the wheel, while I climbed into the passenger seat. After tossing Lucas's clothes into the back, she started the jeep and we were off.

"They're getting closer," she said quietly. "I can sense it. Can't you?"

"Yeah." Even now, I felt as though they were watching.

"How can we make them leave us alone?" Kayla asked.

"I don't know if we can. I think Connor is right. If we destroy the lab, we may slow them down, but I don't think we'll stop them. I guess this isn't exactly how you'd planned to spend your summer vacation."

Kayla released a puff of laughter. "Hardly. I didn't even know Shifters existed when the summer started." She grew serious. "But I'd do anything to protect them now."

"You and me both."

"Do you think we'll win?" she asked.

I didn't answer. I'd met my lie quota for the day. The truth was they were encroaching on our forest, on our lives. I didn't think anything would stop them until they had one of us in their clutches.

NINE

When we got to Tarrant, I gave Kayla directions to my house. I stared at the two-story structure that shouted middle class. My mom had worked hard to buy us that house. I'd always known that I wasn't destined to be the leader of the pack or to even hook up with the leader. I was okay with that. I was okay with the life my mom had given me. Being the best Dark Guardian I could be was the only thing I'd ever wanted. Well, okay, finding my true mate had ranked right up there near the top, but that I couldn't control. Honing my skills as a Guardian—I could.

I grabbed my backpack. "Thanks for the ride."

"We'll be at the Sly Fox tonight," Kayla said. "Come by if you get a chance."

"Yeah, I will. I want to find out what Lucas discovered."

I got out of the jeep and started up the walk, slowing my steps as I heard Kayla drive away. Mom's car was in the driveway so I knew she was home. I saw a curtain at the window flutter. I wondered if Mom was expecting me to shift on my way through the door. We'd always gotten along, even though she thought I needed a life beyond what she saw as my obsession with being a Dark Guardian.

"It isn't everything," she'd often told me.

My usual response had been, "What planet are you from?"

The door didn't spring open. Mom didn't come running out to greet me. Obviously this wasn't going to be a Hallmark moment.

It wasn't until I'd closed the door behind me that Mom rushed forward and crushed me in her embrace. "Oh, baby, are you all right?"

I hated when she called me baby. So juvenile. I hadn't been a baby in a long time. Normally I would have wiggled out of her suffocating embrace, but right at that moment I needed to be held. I was once again fighting back tears. God, these emotions were such a nuisance.

Finally Mom pushed me back, her hands still clutching my shoulders as though she was considering giving me a shake. Her eyes, a green like leaves in spring, stared into mine. Her hair was a reddish brown that I'd always wished she'd passed on to me. I'd never seen a picture of my dad, but she'd told me that I'd taken my dark looks from him.

Mom's anxious eyes filled with sorrow. "You didn't shift."

And my damned eyes filled with tears. "How did you know?" I rasped.

She pulled me close and began to rock me. "Oh, baby, I'm so sorry."

In her voice I heard guilt. I broke free of her hold, crossed my arms over my chest, and glared at her. At least my curiosity had made the tears stop. "For what? What did you do, Mom?"

"Sit down," Mom said.

"I don't need to sit down. Just tell me."

Mom nodded, but she wouldn't meet my eyes. "During the summer I turned seventeen, I went to Europe. I met someone . . . in France. Antonio. I fell in love."

The European Shifter the elders had mentioned. "My dad, right?"

She finally looked at me directly. "Yes. I always told you that he went through the transformation with me— but he didn't."

"So you went through it alone and survived?"

"No, I had a friend. Michael. He went through it with me, but we both knew we were never destined to be mates. And I'd met your father—"

"But he wouldn't go through it with you. So he was what? A total and *complete* loser? Why did you even love him? And what has that got to do with—"

"He was human."

I didn't think a nuclear bomb going off in our living room could have destroyed me more effectively. Black dots danced in front of my vision, and I realized that I had stopped breathing. I wasn't sure I wanted to start up again. But my body that had betrayed me during the last full moon betrayed me again. I dragged in a deep breath.

"You didn't think . . . you didn't"—I'd lost my ability to form coherent thoughts, to speak words—"*that* was worth mentioning before now?"

"I was hoping that you'd never have to know, that you'd inherited my genes, that you'd shift. Especially as you got older and your one dream was to be a Dark Guardian. I didn't want to take that away from you if I didn't have to." She reached for me. "Baby, I—"

"Don't call me that!" I screamed, slapping her hand away. I started to pace around the room. "I'm not a baby. I'm finally a Dark Guardian—but I can't shift. All the work I've done, all the preparation . . ."

"I know. I know how badly you wanted this. I was hoping during this recent trip to Europe that I'd find Antonio, in case you needed him."

I spun around and glared at her. "Why would I need him now?"

"I thought you might need someplace to go. As you neared your time, I never sensed . . ." Her voice trailed off.

"That I was a Shifter?"

She nodded with shame.

"That's just great, Mom. I always thought you were there for me—but when I needed you the most, you weren't. How could you not tell me?"

"I was ashamed. A *human*. No one knows. I never told a soul."

If my own mom was ashamed that she'd hooked up with a human, how did she feel now that she knew for sure her daughter was human? Wouldn't every Shifter's reaction to me if the truth came out be horror? They wouldn't want me. I was no longer one of them.

"I had a right to know." I headed for the door.

"Where are you going?"

"To deal with this the way I've dealt with everything lately—alone."

I felt mean as I trudged toward the Sly Fox. I knew eventually I'd forgive her. We'd talk, and fall back into our odd family roles: Me being the strong one and Mom worrying about things that couldn't be changed. But for now, I was angry, and hurt, and disappointed. In her. And in myself.

My birth date wasn't wrong. My genes were. I was a Static. I was never going to change. And I knew that I couldn't confide what I considered to be a horrible situation to anyone. It wasn't just a reflection on me, but on my mother. Hadn't that been evident in her words as she'd told me about my father?

Whatever Connor might have been feeling last night with our kiss, he'd probably wash his mouth out with soap if he discovered he'd been kissing a Static. I knew I would.

Twilight was settling in. Tarrant was like a little tourist town with cheesy souvenir shops, bed and breakfast inns, and equipment rental places that ran along the main street down the center of town. I wasn't in the mood to deal with tourists so I kept to the back streets that lined the woods. Eventually I'd reach the Sly Fox, which had been built at the edge of town so when it had live bands, no one in town was disturbed. I would meet up with my friends, get lost in the chaos, but until then my mother's revelation was burning itself into the back of my brain.

My head hurt. So did my heart.

Why hadn't I figured it out? Our kind mated for life.

Guys didn't just leave. But like all societies, we had those who didn't conform. I'd thought of my father as the ultimate bad boy who didn't want to be tied down. While it had hurt that he hadn't hung around, I'd fantasized him into being some lonely hero-type. I felt like such an idiot.

I turned down the road that would lead me to the Sly Fox. Connor should be there by now to meet with Lucas. I had a desperate need to see him. I didn't plan to repeat last night, but maybe we could just talk. I could no longer pursue any sort of relationship with him or with any Shifter.

Tomorrow I'd return to Wolford. I'd explain to the elders that I couldn't serve as a Dark Guardian. I wasn't sure yet if I'd tell them the reason. I wasn't even certain my mouth could form the words.

I'm not a Shifter. I'm a Static.

But that fact didn't change the threat to Shifters. I could still help them somehow. I didn't want to walk away when they were in danger.

It was ironic that I wanted to be involved in destroying the one thing that could lead to my salvation. I nearly stumbled over my feet with the thought.

Was what they wanted really so selfish? Or were we the selfish ones? Why not share what we were with the world? If a serum would make me become like all my friends, would I allow it to be injected into my body?

In a heartbeat.

I heard a twig snap. I was too lost in my own thoughts to be alert.

I twisted around just as someone grabbed me, snaking a massive arm around me so I could barely move. I felt a sharp pinprick in my neck. My body instantly went limp and my eyes started fluttering as I struggled to keep them open, as I tried to figure out what had happened.

Then I saw green eyes and brown hair and a triumphant grin. They all came together to form a face I recognized. Mason.

"Don't fight it," he said, almost gently.

But I did. Bio-Chrome was here! I tried to yell for help, but my mouth wouldn't move.

Then the world went black.

The headache that I'd had after I left my mom was ten times worse when I woke up. I wanted to rub my temples, but my hands were tied behind my back. I could feel hard plastic biting into my wrists. And that's when I remembered the needle prick and the other pain: Mason.

My eyes sprung open. I was slumped with my back against a tree, the scent of the rich earth filling my nostrils. I could see plastic-looking things around my ankles. This was so not good.

"Hey, she's up," someone called out.

I glanced over my shoulder to see a Neanderthal-looking guy holding a gun. His head was shaved and he seemed to be in the habit of periodically flexing his muscles as though to draw attention to his amazing biceps. I couldn't see the lights of town, but I could see that the headlights of some vehicle had been strategically placed so I was in the spotlight. This didn't bode well.

I watched as hiking boots came into view and then Mason was crouching in front of me.

"Hey," he said, like we were buddies about to exchange homework answers.

He tugged on my braid. I jerked my head back, trying to break free of his hold. But my hair was too long, and all I accomplished was to give myself a case of whiplash when he jerked me back toward him.

"Play nice," he said.

"Why? You don't."

"Which is why you should." He studied my braid as though he'd never seen hair before. "So is this the color of your fur?"

"You mean the fur that lines my parka? No, it's more a golden brown." My answer made me think of Connor. If I concentrated on him, maybe I could get through this ordeal.

Mason tugged harder.

"Ow!"

"I don't like smart-asses," he said with an edge to his voice that made me wonder if he'd gone off the deep end.

"I don't like stupid questions. My fur? I don't know what you're talking about."

"You're saying you're not a werewolf?"

I rolled my eyes. "You still think they really exist?"

"I know they do. Do you know Devlin?"

Who didn't? He was Lucas's brother. The one who'd betrayed us. He was dead now, but Mason obviously didn't know that. I wasn't about to enlighten him. "Of course, I do. He's a certified nut job."

Mason smiled. "He told me that werewolves live in this area. We caught one. Lucas."

I arched a brow, pleased that I was able to give a cocky façade when I was actually pretty scared. "Lucas is a werewolf? You've, like, what? Seen him go all furry?"

Mason's expression became defensive and mulish. "No, but Devlin told me. And the wolf's fur . . . it was the same shade as Lucas's hair, which you have to admit is a fairly unusual combination of colors."

"Doesn't mean it was Lucas. I mean, really, listen to yourself. Werewolves?"

"I know the sherpas are werewolves. You're a

sherpa, so don't deny it. I know it's how you protect your secrets within the national forest, how you keep outsiders from getting in. You control where campers and hikers can go."

He knew a lot more than I'd given him credit for.

"How many ways can I say this? Werewolves don't exist." It was the mantra Shifters were sworn to repeat. How else could they keep their existence a secret?

"You're going to shift for me, one way or a—"

"She's human," someone said.

Mason twisted around. "Are you sure?"

I looked past Mason to see Ethan striding toward us. He'd been part of the group we'd led into the forest earlier in the summer. He was so pale that we'd pegged him for the indoor type right away but we hadn't thought anything about it since Dr. Keane had claimed he was taking his biology students into the wilderness to study it.

"Blood doesn't lie," Ethan said. "Hers is human."

They'd taken my blood without me knowing? The bastards! I didn't think I'd ever be as grateful as I was at that moment that my mom had slept with a Static.

"But the other one"—Ethan grinned—"bingo!"

"What other one?" I asked, dread tightening my stomach.

With a smile as broad as Ethan's, Mason glanced

over to the side. I followed his gaze. That's when I saw their other prisoner, lying on the ground, with his hands tied behind his back, his ankles bound together, and his eyes closed.

Connor!

TEN

"We've got ourselves a werewolf," Ethan said.

"Are you sure?" Mason asked again.

"Oh yeah. There's a little bit of human, but mostly it's wolf."

I felt everything within me sink into despair.

"You don't seem surprised by the revelation that he's a werewolf," Mason said.

I jerked my gaze up to his. In retrospect, I suppose I should have had some sort of stunned reaction, a gasp, an "Oh my God," but I'd been too worried about Connor. Connor, on the other hand, would have taken offense at being referred to as a werewolf. He was a Shifter. I shored up my bravado. "I'm simply at a loss for words. Your little group is beyond insane—"

He sliced his hand through the air, nearly hitting my nose, cutting off my words. "Save it," he said. "The proof is in the blood."

Which hopefully could be explained away as . . . I didn't know what, but surely as something. That was all they'd ever have. I knew Connor would never shift in front of them. He'd never confirm what they suspected. No matter what they did to him.

My blood suddenly chilled with the thought of what they might have in mind for him.

"All righty, then. Let's pack up," Mason suddenly barked.

"What about the girl?" Neanderthal asked. "Let her go?"

"No," Mason said in a tone that was normally used when addressing idiots. "She'll tell the others. She comes with us. Besides, I have a feeling we can use her to get what we want from the werewolf."

As Neanderthal wrapped his beefy hand around my arm and lifted me to my feet icy fear ripped through me. Connor wasn't the only one in danger. I didn't even want to contemplate what Mason had in mind for me.

They dumped us in the back of the van, slammed the door closed, and locked it. Other doors closed as people got in. Mason looked over the backseat at us. His expression reminded me of hunters admiring the deer they'd shot. "Don't try anything. Johnson here has a stun gun and a tranquilizer gun."

I could see the back of Johnson's head. I wasn't surprised to discover he was the Neanderthal. A guy who could have passed for his twin was driving. Ethan was in the front passenger seat.

"Where are we going?" I asked Mason.

"The lab. It'll make it easier to study wolf boy."

"What is it you want to learn?"

"Didn't Kayla tell you?"

She had, but I was hoping to stall for time. Maybe someone would come across us before they drove off. I gave what I hoped was a pitiful shake of my head.

"Whatever causes him to shift"—he jerked his head toward Connor—"I want to know how it works and re-create it. The ramifications for medicine and the military are astronomical. Not to mention the recreational uses. If you could take a pill and be a werewolf for an hour, wouldn't you?"

I turned my head away because I didn't want him to see how badly I wanted what he might one day be offering.

"Let's go," he said.

The van started up and was soon bouncing over the

road. They had the windows rolled down and the wind whipping through made it difficult to hear their exact words. As much as I strained, all I could hear was the droning of their voices.

Then I heard, "What the f—"

"Shh," I whispered, my face only a couple of inches away from Connor's. There was light coming from the dash, the moon, the stars, maybe even streetlights . . . I didn't know. Or maybe my eyes had just adjusted to the gloom but I could see his features through the shadows.

"Brittany?" he questioned in a low voice.

"Yeah." I saw the whites of his eyes as he rolled them upward, trying to see. "Mason," I said, striving to keep as quiet as possible. With the wind drowning out our voices maybe we could figure out an escape plan without them hearing us.

I could see Connor straining against his bindings. "Save your strength," I suggested.

With a low grunt, he gave up. "I can't believe they got the drop on me."

"I can't either." Surely he would have smelled them before they got too close. "How—"

"They shot me with something."

Thinking of the wolf in the woods, I realized they'd probably used a tranquilizer dart on Connor. I didn't know why they'd decided to take the close approach with me. Maybe they'd run out of darts. I was crushed that they'd overpowered me so easily. Connor had been right. No matter how much I'd prepared, I hadn't been fully prepared.

"Any ideas for how we get out of here?" I asked.

"Guess we try to convince them that we're not werewolves."

They'd already figured that out about me, but Connor didn't know that. I thought about telling him, but I was still reeling from my shame over my mixed parentage. "They tested our blood. It's not human." One truth, one lie. His wasn't human. I wasn't yet ready to say out loud that mine was.

I heard the frustration in his groan. Then I was acutely aware of him shifting, not into wolf, but into warrior mode. His shifting into a wolf might mean he could escape, but it would also confirm for them the existence of our kind. Besides, transforming while he was still bound would have been difficult, and I wasn't certain it would free him from the restraints. I could see him studying our surroundings and recognizing the futility of our present predicament. A time might come when we could escape, but it wasn't now.

"This sucks," Connor hissed beneath his breath. Then he looked at me. "Are you hurt?" His voice reflected genuine concern.

147

"Just my pride."

He flashed a grin, and I was amazed that he was able to do it considering our dire circumstances. "You'll survive."

I thought about the bruising his pride had taken over Lindsey hooking up with Rafe. "We both will."

One way or another.

"How many?" he asked, and I knew he was talking about our captors.

"Four. Mason, Ethan and two badass-looking dudes."

"Must be the hired mercenaries."

Even with the shadows, I could see the determination in Connor's features as he contemplated how best to take them on.

"They have guns," I felt compelled to tell him.

He gave a little nod. He wasn't surprised.

"I think we're stuck here for now, until we reach our destination anyway. They're taking us to the lab."

Connor nodded again, even though I knew he wasn't happy with my assessment. Neither was I but we had to face the reality if we wanted any chance at survival.

I was afraid that Mason might be able to hear us—although it seemed unlikely with the wind rushing through. But I didn't trust him. Connor must have felt the same way because he scooted across the short distance that separated us and pressed his forehead against mine.

"It's going to be okay, Brittany." He brushed his lips across my cheek. The warmth of his nearness chased off the chill of fear that had gripped me ever since I'd realized that Mason had caught Connor as well. I was beyond caring what happened to me, but I didn't want anything bad to happen to Connor.

Especially when we were lying so close together. The timing really sucked but I couldn't help but wonder what might happen if we were alone in this position with no one around and our hands unbound. I imagined him undoing my braid. I could see me shaking out my hair. I envisioned us doing all the things my mother constantly warned me not to do until I was older, until I was in a committed relationship. For this small space of time, with us lying so still, I felt as though anything was possible between us. I wanted so badly to be unbound so I could touch him.

His mouth was so near my lips that if I turned my head just a fraction of an inch we'd be able to kiss. I squeezed my eyes closed. How could I be thinking about us getting intimate when we were in danger of losing our lives? Maybe it was because we *might* die that I suddenly wanted to experience all the passions of life that I hadn't had until now.

I wanted everything: his kiss, his touch . . . *everything*.

We stayed near, our foreheads touching, for what seemed like hours. My body began to ache but I didn't want to move away from Connor to find a more comfortable position. I doubted that one existed anyway. My calf cramped painfully, and I did what little I could to stretch it out. My neck grew stiff.

He was the one in the most danger, because he was what they wanted.

He was a Shifter.

I slept off and on as the hours progressed. I wanted to be rested as much as possible, ready to fight as soon as we could.

The national forest was millions of acres. To drive around it, to get to where the lab was, would take a good part of the night.

It was nearly dawn when the van came to a stop. Doors slammed. Then the back door swung open. Johnson pointed a gun at me. There was a *pop* and a sharp pain spiked in my thigh. I saw the little dart . . .

Fought to keep my eyes open.

Heard Connor roar—

Another pop.

Then everything went black again.

When I woke up, I was lying in a large metal cage in what looked to be a basement. A narrow window high in the cement-block wall allowed in a sprinkling of sunlight. The bars rattled. I rolled over and felt a sense of relief to see that Connor was in the cage with me—testing the strength of our prison. It was tall enough that we could stand up in it, but the door was only half as high. I couldn't figure out how it was secured, but it looked as though it slid up. I imagined Mason and his crew rolling us, unconscious, inside. I got to my feet, wrapped my hands around the bars, and shook the cage. It was sturdy.

Connor hit the bars with the flat of his hand. "It's no use."

He sank down in the corner and draped his hands over his drawn-up knees. He'd obviously woken up before me and checked things out. I slowly looked around. "Any idea what time it is?" I asked.

"No, they took my watch. Probably a strategy Mason learned in Taking Prisoners One-oh-one."

I spied cameras in the corners.

"And yeah, they're watching us," Connor said, not bothering to disguise his disgust.

I swallowed hard and fought to sound brave. "Talk about invasion of privacy."

"I have a feeling our privacy is going to be violated worse than that."

I thought about sitting beside him, but I was too

restless so I paced. "Do you think they can hear us?"

"Not if we talk really quietly."

"I'm really mad at myself," I said through clenched teeth, frustrated. "You warned me to always expect the attack, and I was walking along not paying any atten—"

"Brittany, there's no way we could have anticipated this. You prepare, but in the end—surprise attack always trumps prepared."

I wanted to smile at his attempt to make me feel better. But I knew the truth. I'd been wallowing in my own troubles too much.

"What was it like when they caught you before?" I asked.

He shrugged. "Mason making threats, crowing about how he'd gotten the drop on us. We were in a cave. Who would have thought he'd find us there? The terrain was too rough for a vehicle so they were walking us." He glanced around. "I guess this was supposed to be our final destination."

"Did he do anything?"

"Kept asking us how we shifted. We told him we had no idea what he was talking about." He stared at one of the cameras. "But he just didn't want to listen."

A door opened, the screech of its squeaking hinges indicating that it was heavy. Mason strode in with Ethan, another lab geek we'd met earlier in the summer, and

Tyler, flanking him like idiots who tagged along after the school bully. But behind them were Johnson and his twin, sporting guns. Mason must really fear what Shifters were capable of.

"Good. Sleeping Beauty and her Prince Charming are awake," Mason said, as he and his entourage came to a stop a few feet from the cage. I figured he'd had his eyes glued to a monitor waiting for some sign of activity.

Connor slowly unfurled his body and stood up in the way of a predator that doesn't fear its prey. "Release us, Mason, and we'll let you live."

Mason laughed darkly. "That sounds like a line from a bad movie."

"You must think it's possible that I can take you out or you wouldn't have Dumb and Dumber there with you holding guns."

"What I know is *possible* is this: Werewolves *do* exist. Earlier this summer, we caught Lucas when he was a wolf."

"Yeah," Connor said, mockingly. "I remember you mentioning something about that when you captured me before."

Mason had indeed caught Lucas in wolf form, but he'd never seen him shift in or out of it, so all he had was his belief.

"His fur looked just like Lucas's hair," Mason said,

frustrated anger giving a hard edge to his voice.

"Wolves come in all shades. Check out Wikipedia or Google. They're black, brown, red, gray, white. And some are a combination of all colors. Wolves have been mixing things up for generations. I bet we could even find one that has fur that matches your hair. Let's go take a hike, see what we can find."

"Very funny. I know what I know. Your blood proves it."

"What my blood proves is that someone was careless, mixing samples or something. Or maybe you're just seeing what you want to see."

"Right. Whatever you say." Mason reached back and snapped his fingers. Ethan dropped to the floor like a submissive wolf, opened a case he'd been carrying, and handed Mason a long-handled swab. Mason held it toward Connor. "Need you to swab your mouth. Be sure you get a lot of saliva."

Connor gave him a feral-looking grin and invitingly stepped back. "Come in and swab it yourself."

Mason made a motion with his hand. "Wilson."

Johnson's twin stepped forward and leveled a mean-looking gun on me. My heart hammered my ribs so hard that I was surprised they didn't crack. I angled up my chin in defiance and glared at Mason. "You have totally lost it."

But his attention was focused on Connor. He raised his finger like a teacher making a point. "That, my friend, is not a tranq gun. It's the bullet-holding kind."

"It doesn't matter," I said to Connor, knowing the first time we gave in they'd start making other demands. Surely Mason was bluffing.

With a growl, Connor reached through the bars and snatched the swab from Mason. He twirled it around his mouth and tossed it out. Ethan leaped for it, but he didn't have a Shifter's finely honed reflexes. He scooped it up from the floor.

"Will it be okay?" Mason asked.

"Should be. Just a little dirty." He dropped it into a clear vial.

"Now we want some more blood." Mason tapped the inside of his elbow. "The good stuff."

"Connor—" I began.

"It's just blood." Never taking his eyes from Mason, he shoved up the sleeve of his sweatshirt and pushed his arm between the bars. I figured Connor was imagining how Mason would taste when he finally got his teeth into him. Ethan must have been smart enough to read the murder in Connor's eyes, because he hung back until Mason barked orders at him.

I briefly wondered why Mason hadn't taken any specimens of what he needed while we were unconscious, but then I realized he was striving to make a point here—showing us exactly who was in charge.

I wanted to move closer to Connor, take his hand, but I didn't want to put him in the line of fire—even though the odds of him surviving a bullet were much better than mine. But as long as they never saw Connor shift, all they'd have was lab work that could be disproved some way.

"Impressive guns there," Mason said, referring to Connor's biceps.

"The better to strangle you with."

Mason smirked. "You're just one bad line after another, aren't you?"

"Sorry, but I'm having a hard time taking this little game of yours seriously."

"It's not a game. You'll see. When we have the serum perfected, and I transform into a wolf, maybe you and I will get into it."

"Why wait? Let's get into it now."

"Later. So the muscles, are they a result of the constant transforming?"

"Weights. There is no transforming."

"That line's really getting old. I know what I know."

"Which apparently is nothing."

I could tell that Mason wanted to say more, that he was irritated with Connor's attitude. As for me, I was

impressed that he could act so cool and nonchalant—like
our lives weren't in danger of ending at any moment.

When Ethan was finished drawing blood, he took
some of Connor's hair and a scraping of his skin. He
looked unsure as he covered the bleeding spot on the back
of Connor's hand with a bandage. When Ethan moved
away with his treasures, Tyler approached with a cooler.
He started placing bottled water between the bars.

"What? No beer?" Connor asked sarcastically.

It was hard to believe now that earlier in the summer
we'd all drunk beer together out in the woods.

Tyler's cheeks burned red, but he didn't say anything
as he also placed prepackaged sandwiches, protein bars,
and some apples inside the cage.

"All right," Mason said. "Enjoy your meal. We'll be
in touch." He turned to go.

"Hey, Mason," Connor called out lightly, like one
buddy to another.

Mason swung back around.

"You really don't want me for an enemy," Connor
said darkly, in a threatening manner that even sent a
shiver of dread up my spine.

Mason paled before regaining his cocky composure.
"Same goes."

Not until Mason and his entourage had left the room
did I hurry over and wrap my arms around Connor. He

closed his around me, squeezing me tightly. Not since I'd faced the moon alone had I felt so terrified.

"At least they didn't take anything from you," Connor said quietly.

I squeezed my eyes shut. There was a reason they hadn't, but I couldn't bring myself to tell him that I wasn't a Shifter and they knew it. I really wasn't rooting for the bad guys to come out victorious in all this, but I also couldn't help thinking that if Mason did succeed, if he did develop a serum or a pill or whatever—that if I took it, Connor would never have to know about my deficiencies. Instinctively I knew that it was the bond of Shifters that was driving him toward me. He thought we were the same species. Shifters moved around in packs. Even out in the world, Shifters kept their distance, were wary of non-Shifters. I still couldn't believe my mom had fallen in love with a human.

"Everything's going to be okay," Connor assured me.

Tilting my head back, I studied the contours of his face, saw no doubt in his eyes. "How can you be so sure?"

"Because I know when our opportunity comes to escape you'll be able to kick his butt."

Releasing a strangled laugh, I fought not to start crying like a human girl would. I wanted to be Shifter-strong for Connor.

Tenderly he cradled my cheek and leaned in, his lips brushing near my ear as he spoke in an incredibly low and sensual voice. "Seriously. We won't be alone for long. We just have to hold on until the others get here."

"How do you know they'll come?" I whispered.

"Because my team was supposed to come scout this area out, and when I don't show up, they'll get Lucas. Might take them a couple of days of trying to figure out where the hell I went, but eventually the pack comes first and they'll head up here to complete their mission. And rescue us in the process."

I knew the timing was lousy, but when would be a better time? I was still stinging from his decision to oust me. "Why did you kick me off your team?"

Leaning back, he stroked his thumb over my bottom lip. "Because I can't concentrate when you're around. Because from the moment you silently challenged me in the dungeon, whenever I see you I feel that punch to the gut Lucas was talking about and all I want is—"

He kissed me with a hunger, a desperation. Maybe our fears that we weren't in control as much as we were used to added to the moment. But we clung to each other as though we never planned to let go. In the back of my mind, I knew this was a bad idea. It was just going to give Mason more fuel to use against us.

Connor must have had the same thought, because he drew back and squinted at one of the cameras. "Bad timing."

"It always is with us, I guess."

Again he brushed his thumb over my lower lip, but it was swollen now and tingled. "Yeah. I'm hungry, and not just for you."

He started to step away, then stopped. "Hey, what's that?"

I followed the direction of his gaze and discovered a tear in the sleeve of my shirt. "They must have torn my shirt getting me into the cage or something. No big deal."

"Not that," he said, his voice taut. He slipped his finger inside the ragged tear. "*That.* Did Mason hurt you?"

And I realized he'd spotted the bruise he'd given me when we wrestled. But I couldn't admit that. He'd wonder why I hadn't taken care of it the Shifter-way.

"Yeah, I guess. But it's not bad. It doesn't bother me."

"That guy's gonna pay," he ground out, releasing my arm, but taking my hand. He pulled me down to the floor and we sat against the bars. He opened one of the bottles of water and sniffed it. He handed it to me.

"You think it's safe?" I asked.

"I can't smell anything that shouldn't be there. Worst case scenario, they added something to the water or food to put us to sleep. Quite honestly, I think Mason would have more fun shooting us with tranq guns. He's not exactly Mr. Subtle when it comes to his plans. Seriously

160

he's just trying to be in control."

I grinned. "I like that you think he's just *trying*."

"Hey, I've seen enough creature features to know the good guys always win."

"You're not afraid at all, are you?"

Instead of answering, he reached for a sandwich.

ELEVEN

Be careful what you wish for, my mother had always warned me. I'd wanted time alone with Connor and now I had it.

The hours of sunlight dragged by. We weren't convinced mikes weren't around somewhere to pick up our conversations, so unless we wanted to talk with our mouths pressed to each other's ear we avoided discussing anything that might make Mason think he was on the right track. Further lab work was probably going to confirm that Connor was a Shifter—but we still held out hope that it could be explained away if that was all they had.

We were sitting in opposite corners, because we didn't want our passion captured on video either and it was difficult to be close and not give in to temptation.

"Best movie of all time?" I asked.

"*300*. Definitely. You?"

"*Shawshank Redemption*."

His mouth dropped. "You're kidding. Were we even born when it came out?"

"I've seen it on video."

He grinned. "I should have known you wouldn't pick a chick flick. It's actually second on my list."

"And you're giving me a hard time about it?"

He nodded toward the window. "We have a lot of sunlight to get through."

I glanced around. Smaller, empty cages were stacked along one of the walls. "You think they made this room just for us?"

"I think they thought they were going to have lots of specimens."

"Do you believe this serum Mason is talking about—what he wants it to do—do you believe it's even possible?"

"I suck at biology. But if I had to guess"—he slowly shook his head—"Warning: mad scientist at work."

I nodded. I didn't know whether to be disappointed or have hope. Whatever was finally developing between

Connor and me—would it come to a screeching halt if I told him the truth?

"Favorite TV series," he prodded as though he could tell my thoughts were drifting toward places they shouldn't.

"24."

He grinned as though immensely pleased. "Action girl."

I shrugged, a little embarrassed that my answers probably didn't fall in line with the typical girl's. "What can I say? Give me a few explosions along with some unlikely situations and I'm happy."

"I feel for Bauer. He never gets a chance to eat or sleep."

"I like that no matter where he needs to be, he's only five minutes away."

Connor laughed. It was a deep, throaty sound. I wouldn't have thought I could actually enjoy our situation.

"We must be driving Mason crazy," I said.

"Why? Because we're not prowling around like the animals he thinks we are?"

"Because we're acting like we're having a good time."

"I am having a good time." He picked at the bandage. It probably irritated him that he couldn't shift and heal the scrape. "It's kinda funny, but I never had quiet moments with Lindsey. We were always busy, always doing something. Don't get me wrong. I had fun doing things with her." He looked over at me. "But it's fun just doing *nothing* with you."

"I'm going to pretend that's a compliment."

"It's definitely a compliment. I'd come over there and give you more than that if it wouldn't give Mason a thrill."

I couldn't stop myself from blushing and smiling at the same time. "I think he needs a girlfriend."

"Good luck with that. She'd have to be totally oblivious to what a nutcase he is."

Every now and then Connor worked in a jab, just in case Mason was listening. I could envision him gritting his teeth as he listened through headphones.

"Where do you think his dad is?" I asked.

Connor shrugged. "I always had the impression that Mason was the driving force behind this venture. His dad just hung around to provide authority."

"Kayla said Mason is a genius. He's not much older than we are, but he's already finished with college, working in the Bio-Chrome lab."

"The guy definitely needs a life."

Which I figured was what prompted him to search for a way to transfer a Shifter's abilities to himself.

We returned to our little game of bests. It was interesting learning about Connor's likes: favorite spectator sport—baseball; favorite participator sport—basketball; favorite food: rare sirloin.

Shadows were beginning to creep in—the sun was setting. We soon heard the clank of the door unlocking. Monique came in, pushing a silver cart.

She, too, had been part of the Bio-Chrome group that we'd led into the wilderness. She was lithe, graceful, with milk-chocolate skin and a flawless complexion. She'd seemed nice enough when we first met her, but looking at her now, I had to wonder what kind of person she was to get mixed up in this madness.

"Hey, guys. It's great to see you again," she said with patently false cheer, bringing the cart to a halt. "I've brought you a little dinner."

She pushed a button on a handheld gadget and the door rose slightly. She shoved two covered plates through the narrow opening.

Connor took one and lifted the lid to reveal sirloin, rare, and what I'd told him was my favorite vegetable, even though I seldom ate it because it was so unhealthy—crispy, golden fries.

"Cute, so Mason wants us to know he's listening," Connor said. He raised a brow at Monique. "Knife and fork?"

She smirked. "Nice try, but we figure you'd find some way to use them to escape or hurt us. I did bring you some napkins, little ketchup packets, and some more water."

She shoved everything else into our cage and promptly closed the door.

"Any chance we could get some blankets?" Connor asked. "It's gonna get cold in here tonight."

Her lovely features reflected regret. "I'm sorry. I wish I could bring you some. If you get cold, you'll just have to go all furry."

I glared at her. "And when we turn blue? Are you going to come in here and revive us?"

"Snuggle up. He can keep you warm."

"I didn't expect you to be such a cold bitch," I said.

"Look, guys, I'm just paid to do a job. Cooperate and it'll go easier for all of us. Then we can all go home. I've got zero social life out here." With that, she marched out.

I moved over, sat next to Connor, and took the plate he offered. "The least they could have done was cut it up," I muttered.

"They probably expect us to tear into it with our powerful bite."

I sighed. "This is getting old fast."

* * *

167

The darkness arrived, and with it the chill of the night. Maybe because they planned to house animals here they hadn't spent money to hook this part of their lab up to a heater. Or maybe—more likely—they simply weren't turning it on because they hoped to force us—or Connor, in any case—into shifting.

After we'd finished eating, we didn't continue to play games. We retreated to our respective corners and became lost in our own thoughts. A little moonlight spilled in. I wondered if we'd still be here when the dark of the moon arrived, when the moon wasn't visible in the night sky. I unbraided my hair so it could serve as a flimsy blanket over my shoulders. I crossed my arms over my chest and held them tightly against my body striving to hold in as much warmth as possible. I closed my eyes. Maybe if I imagined a large log fire in the middle of a clearing, sparks shooting up, flames writhing—

I heard movement and opened my eyes. Connor was crouched beside me. I knew I couldn't see him as clearly as he could see me, but there was enough moonlight for me to make out the shadows of his features.

"Here, you can wear my sweatshirt," he began, reaching for the ends.

I grabbed his arm to stop him. "While you turn cold? I can't do that."

"Come on, Brit. I can hear your teeth chattering

from over there. Besides, my body temperature is off. I'm always hot."

He'd never shortened my name before. It somehow seemed more intimate. "Okay. Thanks."

I drew his shirt on over my head. It was incredibly soft and still carried his warmth and scent. For a few minutes at least, my shivering ceased.

Connor sat beside me, slid one arm beneath my knees, the other around my back, and pulled me onto his lap.

"What are you doing?" I asked.

"Press as much of you against me as you can. It'll help generate some heat."

I wrapped my arms around his chest and buried my face in the curve of his neck.

"Ah, your nose is cold," he said.

I jerked back. "Sorry."

He released a low chuckle, placed his hand on my cheek, and guided me back. "It's okay. It'll warm up."

I inhaled his earthy scent.

"You know what would really generate heat?" he asked after a while, then provided the answer. "If we made out."

"You don't think Mason would post the video on YouTube?"

"Yeah, he probably would. Or he'd threaten to if we

didn't meet his demands. Course, the images might not be very clear in the dark like this."

"Why do you think he hasn't turned on the lights?" I'd noticed them in the ceiling that afternoon.

"Maybe they can't. Maybe they haven't paid their electric bill."

"No, seriously. Why is he keeping us in the dark?"

"Probably thinks we'll do things in the dark that we wouldn't do in the light." He nuzzled my neck, and I heard him inhaling my scent. "You smell good."

"I don't see how I can."

"The essence of you, the unique part of you that no one else smells like. The part that lets a predator track you." The entire time he talked, his mouth breathed warm air over my skin. "You smell like"—he inhaled deeply again—"mint leaves when they're crushed."

"You smell like the forest: rich, pungent, and powerful."

"I like that."

He skimmed his lips along my jaw and then we were kissing, generating heat that rivaled that of a furnace. When we were this close, I wasn't afraid of what tomorrow might bring. All that mattered was now.

"Tell me I'm not a rebound girl," I ordered when we came up for air.

"You're not a rebound. You could never be a rebound."

We were kissing again. His hand sneaked up and rested flat against my stomach. How could it be so warm when my hands were still cold?

When his mouth left mine to taste the curve of my neck, I said, "You never noticed me before."

He stilled as though he needed to think about it. "I noticed. I just didn't pay attention to what I was noticing."

"Maybe what we're feeling here, between us, is Stockholm Syndrome or something. Maybe we're reacting to the situation. I've heard when hostages—"

"We're not hostages. And what's happening between us, what I'm feeling for you"—he cradled my face between both of his hands—"it started long before Mason shot me with a tranquilizer dart. I was heading away from the Sly Fox, heading to your house, because I needed to see you, I needed to explain . . . what I feel for you, Brit, it's so much more powerful than anything I've ever felt for *anyone*. And yeah, I'm not quite comfortable with it, but I want to explore it. See where it leads."

It sounded as though he was talking about falling in love. I gave him a crooked smile and a shaky nod. Then we were kissing again.

For tonight at least, I thought we'd stay warm.

I woke up in the morning with Connor's body resting over mine, shielding me from the cold. I ran my hands over his back, felt the chill on his skin, and began rubbing vigorously.

"Feels good," he mumbled.

We'd spent a good deal of the night kissing, hugging, and talking. Until we'd finally drifted off to sleep in each other's arms. I lifted my head and nipped his shoulder with my teeth.

"Hey, watch it." He nuzzled just below my ear. "Remember, Shifter bites take longer to heal and they scar."

All playfulness left me. I could bite him all day long, but with one quick shift all evidence would fade away. I knew I needed to tell him the truth about me, but I didn't want to lose this fragile bond that was developing. I'd wanted it too long and too much to risk it now.

But I knew the closer we became, the harder it would be to keep my secret.

"You know what I want?" he whispered in a low, sexy voice.

"What?"

"To shift with you."

I went so incredibly still it was a wonder my heart still beat. He lifted himself up, grinned at me, and stroked my cheeks. "Hey, don't look so scared. I know it won't be anything like your first time, but if we wait for a full moon and make it special, it could still create the bond."

I licked my lips, my heart breaking for what I couldn't give him. "We probably shouldn't be talking about this now."

His brow furrowed. "Yeah, you're probably right. Sorry. Didn't mean to rush things."

He started to get up and I locked my arms around his neck, holding him in place. "No, it's not that. I swear to you, Connor, there's nothing I want more."

He grinned. "Okay, then. It's settled. But first things first, right? We gotta get the hell out of here."

I nodded. Yeah, that was a priority. Then I could face destroying us with the truth about me.

TWELVE

Monique brought us breakfast. Funny thing was, she appeared really nervous doing it and wouldn't even look at us directly.

"I'll see if I can find you some blankets for tonight," she said quietly before leaving.

"What was that about?" I asked as I ate the sausage and biscuit. "Do you think watching us last night embarrassed them?"

Connor shook his head. "I don't see how. I mean, yeah, we got a little carried away with the kissing, but we didn't go nearly as far as I wanted."

I felt my cheeks warm, broke off a bit of biscuit, and

tossed it at him. "Bad boy."

"I'm gonna be if we don't get out of here." Finished with his meal, he brushed off his hands and began walking slowly around the perimeter of the cage. "There has to be a way out."

"Once we get out of the cage, we have to get through a locked door."

He winked at me. "One prison at a time."

The door opened and Mason strode in with his familiar entourage and two guys I didn't know. They were beefier than the lab guys, but not quite as buff as the ones holding guns.

"Ah, company," Connor said. "And here I am not yet dressed."

I was still wearing his sweatshirt.

"That's okay," Mason said. "So what's the ink on your back mean? I know Lucas and Rafe have one."

"Fraternity initiation."

Which was what Rafe had told Mason earlier in the summer when he'd asked.

"See, I don't believe it. However, that's okay. Studying the samples you provided yesterday has proved very enlightening. But what I really want is to see you transform into a wolf."

"Afraid you're just going to have to be disappointed, because I can't transform."

"Can't or won't?" Mason asked.

"Don't you think if I had the ability to change into a wolf, I'd have done it when you captured me before? You know, when I was escaping?"

"Wolves invaded our camp. Are you saying you're a wolf whisperer?"

"I'm saying I'm not a werewolf."

Mason grinned. "One way to find out for sure."

I heard clanking and glanced over to where Ethan, Tyler, and the two new guys were building what looked like a metal tunnel. I was dying to ask Mason what was going on, but I wouldn't give him the satisfaction.

Connor must have realized that Mason had something unpleasant planned, because he moved over, wrapped his hand around mine, and squeezed. I squeezed back.

"What do you think he has planned?" I asked.

"I don't know, but I don't like it."

They shoved the tunnel over until one open end covered the doorway of our cage. I heard the squeaking of wheels and watched as a cage was rolled in—a cage housing a cougar.

"Damn," Connor muttered.

"Is he a Shifter?" I whispered. Some of our kind shifted into other animal forms.

Connor shook his head. "No, he's the real deal."

I was grateful that he didn't question why I couldn't

sense the truth about the cougar. I figured he was too busy thinking strategy. Unfortunately, if what I thought was about to happen happened—he had only one option.

They set the cage in front of the other end of the tunnel and secured it.

Connor glared at Mason. "Mason."

The threat in his voice was unmistakable.

"It's for the good of mankind."

"That's bullshit. All you want is to be something you're not. You want it so much you're willing to believe something this crazy, go this far, to get it."

"If I don't personally benefit, then it doesn't make me the bad guy."

What a lie! We already knew he had plans to personally benefit.

"Read my lips," Connor said. "Look into my eyes. I'm not a werewolf. If you let that cougar in here, he's going to kill us."

For a split second, a single heartbeat, Mason seemed unsure. Then he shook his head, nodded as though he'd been arguing with himself. "I know what I know," he said sternly.

"At least take Brittany out of here, so you don't have two deaths on your hands."

"She's my guarantee you'll fight and not surrender,"

Mason said, and at that moment I hated him with every fiber of my being.

"Oh God," I whispered as Mason pointed the remote and our door slowly opened.

Connor released a harsh curse, and I knew he'd been bluffing, that he wouldn't willingly accept death on Mason's terms. Still, I was terrified at the thought of what was about to happen.

Connor jerked off a boot and threw it at the bars. He did the same with the other.

I moved back, leaving him room to maneuver. His socks came off next and then he was reaching for his belt.

The door to the other cage began opening. The cougar snarled, the catlike sound grating on my ears, setting my teeth on edge. My back hit the corner, rattling the cage.

Connor jerked his attention over to me. "Brittany, get ready to shift."

I shook my head, tears burning my eyes. "I can't."

"What?" Connor took a step toward me, flinging his hand out to where Mason and the others stood. "Forget them, ignore them. This is our survival we're talking about. I might be able to take him, but if he gets a shot at you, you're in a better position to defend yourself as a wolf."

I knew I had to kill any hope he had that we were in

this together. "I can't shift. I'm so sorry, Connor, but I'm not a Shifter. I'm human."

They were the hardest words I'd ever spoken. And judging by the stunned expression on Connor's face they were the worst words he'd ever heard.

The cougar shrieked as it loped down the tunnel. Connor's survival instincts kicked in. He backed into the far corner to give himself maneuverability and began to remove his jeans.

I turned away, wrapping my hands around the bars, because I couldn't stand to watch the confrontation. The cage shook with the power of the cougar entering it and then I heard the howl of the wolf.

I spun around. The wolf and cougar were entangled in a deadly embrace, similar to what Connor and I had experienced when we'd wrestled. First one would be on top, then the other. Then they'd break apart and come at each other again. Teeth and claws were striking hard, making wounds, drawing blood that was beginning to leave trails on the floor.

My gaze drifted over to Mason once. He looked as though he was experiencing ecstasy. I could see the hunger, the yearning to possess the power that Connor now exhibited.

But mostly I watched Connor fighting for his life, knowing there was little I could do. I had no weapon.

I had no way to help him maneuver the cougar into a position that would allow him to sink his teeth into its throat. I jumped around the cage, trying not to get in the way, thinking that if I could get to the doorway, I could scamper into the tunnel and give Connor more room to fight without having to worry about me.

As though he was now worrying about me. He was probably wishing the cougar had taken me first as a snack.

Suddenly I was angrier than I'd ever been. Angry at my mother for leading me to believe that I was a Shifter. Angry at Mason for forcing me to reveal that I wasn't. I wanted to take him on.

Then I thought to hell with him and his manipulations. Just because I wasn't a Shifter, it didn't mean that Connor had to fight alone. I had a mean roundhouse kick.

Making fists, bouncing on the balls of my feet, I concentrated on the battle playing out before me, waiting for the moment to make my strike. I knew Connor's moves, had experienced them firsthand. His wolf maneuvers wouldn't be that different, because even in wolf form he was still Connor. I watched, saw the opportunity, moved in, and kicked the cougar's rump—hard.

Hard enough to make it screech. Hard enough to distract it.

I quickly backed off.

Connor had an advantage now and he took it. Went in for the kill, sank his teeth into the cougar's jugular.

I knew, unlike Mason, Connor took no pleasure in ending any creature's life. Shifters respected all aspects of nature. Even an enemy was killed with regret.

The cougar thrashed and stilled. Connor backed away, stumbled, and went down. Until that moment, I hadn't realized that he'd been seriously wounded.

I rushed over to him, knelt beside him, and gently lifted his head into my lap.

When Shifters transformed, hair turned into fur, hands and feet became paws, teeth sharpened and lengthen, noses turned into snouts—but the eyes, the eyes didn't change. When someone looked into the eyes of a Shifter, he saw human eyes, not wolf eyes.

So now as I gazed at the wolf's face, I was looking into Connor's eyes. It was Connor I was seeing, Connor I was talking to. "I'm so sorry. I should have told you." I combed my fingers through his fur. "I'm so, so sorry." I knew I was repeating myself but I couldn't think of any other words to express my sorrow and remorse. And my shame.

I'd let him down. Something I'd never expected to do. No matter the circumstances, I'd always thought I could protect our kind, I could uphold my end of any confrontation.

I heard movement and glanced up. Mason and Wilson were standing by the cage, Wilson pointing a dart gun. I held up my hand. "No, you have to give him time—"

Wilson fired. Connor jerked as the dart lodged home in his shoulder. He struggled to lift his head, but in his eyes I could see the drug taking effect. He collapsed in my lap.

"Damn you, Mason! You needed to give him time to heal." I tore off the sweatshirt and by the time I draped it over Connor, he had returned to human form.

"Huh," Mason said. "So they revert back when they're unconscious?"

I wasn't in the mood to answer his questions. Blood was soaking through the shirt. "He's badly hurt. He needs a doctor."

"You're not a werewolf, but you know about werewolves." He was stating not asking.

"Shifters. They refer to themselves as Shifters. Get him a doctor and I'll tell you everything I know."

"No lies?"

"No lies."

He nodded and glanced over his shoulder. "Ethan, go get my dad."

I wouldn't leave until Dr. Keane was finished treating Connor. Since I'd last seen him, his hair had gone completely white. I imagined working with his out-of-control son could do that to a man.

"So I just stitch him up normally, as though he were human?" Dr. Keane asked.

I confirmed his question with a nod. Connor's head was in my lap and I was combing my fingers through his hair. The cougar had gotten him in the shoulder, side, and thigh. "When he wakes up, he'll heal himself."

"So he can shift at will," Mason said. "Not just when danger threatens. I mean, he doesn't need an adrenaline rush to trigger the change?"

"He shifts at will," I confirmed, feeling sick to my stomach with each fact I corroborated.

"When we shot Lucas with a tranq dart, he didn't shift back."

"Maybe he wasn't completely unconscious."

"So Lucas *is* the wolf with the multicolored coat."

I hated that I'd unwittingly betrayed Lucas by not paying more attention to the questions. Yes, I'd promised to tell Mason everything, but I was only planning to tell him *everything* that wouldn't give him any sort of advantage over the Shifters. I may not be one of them but my loyalty first and foremost was to them. "Yes."

"So are only the male sherpas Shifters?" Mason asked.

I swallowed hard. "No, there are girls."

"But not you?"

I shook my head.

"Our tests have already proven it's genetic, and Connor thought you were a Shifter so what's the story there?"

I didn't figure I had anything to lose so I told him about my Shifter mother and human father.

"Then the Shifter gene is recessive," he said.

I shrugged. "You're the scientist, not me."

"Has to be; otherwise there'd be more Shifters than humans."

"Maybe you just don't recognize a Shifter when you see him." I couldn't prevent the snide comment from slipping out but regretted it as soon as Mason said, "You know we can rip those stitches right out of Connor. We could even inflict some more wounds if we wanted, worse wounds."

I gritted my teeth. "Humans outnumber Shifters."

"Thank you. See how easy it is when we all cooperate?"

Thank God, he didn't ask any more questions until I was satisfied with the work his dad had done on Connor. It wasn't the prettiest stitching I'd ever seen, but it wasn't as though I planned to frame it and hang it on the wall. It just needed to do its job—stop the bleeding until Connor woke up and could tend to his own wounds.

To my immense shock, Mason let me take a shower to wash off all the blood. Monique served as my bodyguard and stayed in the bathroom to make sure I didn't try to make a run for it. But her presence was totally unnecessary. I wasn't going to leave Connor.

"You know I never really believed it was possible," Monique called through the shower curtain. "The ability to change into another shape. It just seemed so improbable, something better suited to the SciFi channel."

Scrubbing my body hard, I didn't answer.

"But the pay was so good, you know? I'm the oldest of seven. My parents aren't well-off. I was trying to do what I could to help out."

If she was seeking forgiveness for her part in this experiment, she was looking in the wrong place.

Monique was taller than I was but sweats are somewhat adjustable so she let me borrow a pair that she never used in public, but used solely for hanging around her house. She liked them large so she'd be comfy. What was loose on her was snug on me.

She also located some blankets and borrowed a sweatshirt from Johnson that I could take to Connor. Not that I thought he'd wear it. It had the Bio-Chrome logo imprinted above their slogan: "Studying chromosomes for a better tomorrow."

"When you brought us breakfast this morning, you knew what they had planned," I said.

She appeared remarkably sad when she nodded. "Yeah. For what it's worth, we all thought it was a bad idea—but Mason is obsessed with the medical ramifications. Don't you understand the lives that we could save?"

"The Shifters don't hold the cure. Do you really believe you can transfer abilities that easily? There are creatures with the ability to regenerate missing limbs. Do you think they'd provide us with that capability if we sucked the life out of them and put them in a test tube?"

"They're not as similar to us as the werewolves are."

"Shifters," I corrected her.

I expected her to take me to an interrogation room like I'd often seen in movies: one table, one hard chair, a dim light bulb hanging from a cord.

Instead she took me into an opulent room that was all white furniture and black décor. Mason and his father were sitting in large, plush chairs. Wilson and Johnson were standing nearby, tranq guns at the ready. Maybe they were worried that I'd try to overpower them. But all I wanted was to get this interview over and get back to Connor.

Mason indicated the sofa. "Make yourself comfortable."

After everything that had happened, this moment was

surreal. I tried not to moan at the luxurious comfort that enveloped me when I sat. It was a sharp contrast to the concrete floor on which I'd spent the night and Connor was now lying.

"Help yourself," Dr. Keane said, waving his hand over the coffee table in front of me where tiny bubbles rose through the liquid in a champagne flute and appetizers waited on black plates.

"Let's just get this done," I said impatiently, anxious to get back to Connor—even though he probably had no desire to see me return now that he knew the truth about me.

"All right." Mason leaned forward. "So Shifters are born."

"Yes."

"Do they always have the ability to shift?"

"No."

He arched a brow at my reticent answer. "Explain."

"The ability to shift is dormant until the girl turns seventeen and the guy turns eighteen. During the first full moon following the designated birthday, the first shift occurs. It can't be stopped. It can't be controlled. After that, a Shifter learns to shift at will."

"Is everyone in Tarrant a Shifter?"

"No." We had a lot of tourists, campers, and nature buffs who came through, so it wasn't a lie.

"The tattoos I've seen—what do they signify?"

"Shifters are connected to wolves and wolves mate for life. When a guy finds his mate, he has a Celtic symbol representing her name—or as close to it as possible—inked on his shoulder. It's tradition."

"Celtic. Are your origins in Great Britain?"

"We don't know for sure. We think so, but . . ." This was hard. Telling him so much.

"But?" he prodded.

"Shifters live all over the world. Different clans."

"Are they all wolf?"

"No, but I've never seen one that wasn't."

"So the different animals don't mix?"

I shrugged. "I don't know. I just know I've never seen one."

"Interesting." He ran his fingers over his face as though he could see it changing into that of a wolf. His actions gave me the creeps.

He narrowed his eyes in thought. "So what are the sherpas protecting in the forest?"

"Little hidey holes like the cave where you found Connor and the others a couple of weeks ago."

"That's it?" he asked in disbelief.

"Isn't that enough?"

"I thought maybe there was a village or a secret city."

No way was I going to tell him about Wolford. "Shifters are nature lovers. They like to hang out in forests. As you saw with Connor, clothes come off when they shift so they have areas where they hide things—extra food, clothes. That sort of thing."

He leaned forward, his eyes searching my face. "Tell me everything you know that I haven't asked."

I wasn't going to reveal that when in wolf form, a Shifter could communicate telepathically with other Shifters who were also in wolf form. That was Connor's secret weapon. It was the only chance he had to save himself. The only chance the Shifters had to possibly stop word of their existence from reaching beyond Bio-Chrome.

But I knew I had to give him something. "The first time a guy transforms, he goes through it alone. But a girl always has her mate with her. If she doesn't, she'll die."

"Why?"

"I have no idea. Maybe it's some sort of evolutionary thing. Could have an impact on your experiments."

He gave me a smile that made me feel as though I had ants crawling over my skin, as though I was suddenly one of his team, part of his inner group. "That's good info to know. Thanks, Brittany."

"Can I go now?"

"Yeah, sure. You'll be staying in Monique's room with her."

"No, I want to go back to Connor."

"Why would you want to go back to a cage with a cement floor and no comforts? Besides, didn't you see the way Connor looked at you? He was disgusted."

I had seen it. It was part of the reason that I needed to get back to him, to try to explain. And if he still hated me, it wouldn't be any more than I hated myself at that moment. "Come on, Mason. Let me go back. I told you everything I know."

"Everything?"

"Everything."

"Then what do you have to bargain with?"

Mason and I dickered back and forth until we finally made one more deal. It would either bring me happiness . . . or death.

THIRTEEN

With his entourage in tow, Mason led me back to the prison room, his hand wrapped around my arm as though he thought I'd try to run off. I was carrying the blankets and sweatshirt that Monique had given me. The sun was setting, the shadows easing back in.

Connor was sitting up in the cage, his jeans on, the only sign of his earlier wounds the bloodied sweatshirt that he'd managed to throw out between the bars. It was a rumpled heap on the floor. With his arms crossed over his bare chest, he glared at us as we approached.

"So you've healed yourself," Mason said.

Connor simply continued to glare.

"What? No witty comeback?" Mason prodded.

If looks could kill, Mason would have died on the spot in two seconds flat.

"I know my measures were a bit extreme, but we're making remarkable progress and I needed to know if what we're seeing in the lab ferrets when we inject them with the serum is how it's supposed to work."

I jerked my head around to stare at him. "You're turning ferrets into wolves?"

He held up a finger and thumb with a small amount of space between them. "Very small wolves. Sometimes it works, sometimes it doesn't." He tapped his head. "I'm thinking it's the consciousness that makes the difference. You have to be able to think wolf to be wolf."

"We've only been here a couple of days, and you already have a serum?" I was flabbergasted. He hadn't told me they were that close to perfecting the serum.

"We've been working on the formula for a long time. We just had a few missing pieces. And now that we have those our puzzle is almost complete." He turned his attention back to Connor. "I need to put her back in the cage, and I want to do it with as little trouble as possible. I have to open the door to do that. If you move a quarter of an inch toward it, Wilson will zap you."

Connor didn't move. Not even an eighth of an inch.

Once I crawled inside, the door to our prison clanged shut.

"Enjoy what little time you have together," Mason said.

I stood up. "What are you talking about?"

"All good things must come to an end."

"What does that mean?"

Ignoring me, he strode from the room, his little groupies trailing along behind him. I smacked my palm against the bars. "Son of a bitch."

I wrapped my hands around the cold metal and pressed my forehead against it. I'd thought I was prepared to face Connor but I wasn't prepared for the fury emanating from him. I had so much to explain and I didn't know where to begin. Taking a deep breath, I reached down and picked up the bundle I'd dropped earlier.

I turned around. Connor was in the exact same position.

"I brought you a clean sweatshirt, and now we have some blankets."

He studied me as though he had no idea who I was. I guess he really didn't.

"But I guess what you really want is a Shifter, isn't it?"

Slowly he uncrossed his arms. He drew up one knee and draped his wrist over it, but he wasn't nearly as relaxed as he was trying to appear because both fists were balled so tightly that his knuckles were turning white. "When did you know you weren't?"

Hearing his voice was like a gentle stroke across my heart. The words held no warmth, but neither were they ice. They were neutral as though he was testing things out as much as I was. I clutched the blankets. "During the full moon. It came. It went. I stayed the same. Not even a tingle. The night Mason got a jump on me, I was distracted. I'd just talked to my mom. She told me my dad was some guy she met in Europe." I laughed bitterly. "Some human guy. All these years when she said he went through her transformation with her, then left . . . it was just a lie. She went through it with some guy named Michael. But he didn't stay around either." My mom and I seemed to have that in common—guys wouldn't commit to us.

His gaze wandered slowly over me. Once. Twice. Three times.

"Say something," I demanded.

"You smell like Monique."

"They let me use her shower. These are her clothes. Your blood was on mine." This conversation was so inane. Why didn't he yell at me? Shout? Tell me how much he hated me?

Watching him was too hard. I started to look around

194

when my eyes were arrested by the mangled bent bars on the side near where he was sitting. "What happened there? Did that happen during the fight with the cougar?" It must have but I'd been too preoccupied with other things to notice.

"No."

I gave my attention back to him. "Then *what*?"

He slowly unfolded his body in that predatory way he had and came forward until he was standing in front of me. Again his gaze wandered over me. He inhaled my scent, shook his head. "How could I have not known? Why didn't any of us recognize the truth about you?"

I took a shaky breath. "I don't know. Maybe I have just enough of my mother in me to fool everyone."

He touched his knuckles to my cheek. "All these years, you believed you were a Shifter?"

I nodded. How could I even begin to explain? How could he possibly understand?

"After the full moon, you must have been—"

"Devastated."

He put his arms around me, drew me close. I absorbed his warmth and his strength. Took the comfort he offered.

I didn't know how long he held me. Eventually, when we sat down, he pulled me onto his lap and kept his arms around me.

"So what happened to the cage?" I finally asked.

"When I woke up and you weren't here, I went berserk trying to get out, so I could kill Mason."

"Oh my God, Connor, I'm so sor—"

"Will you stop apologizing for things that aren't your fault? I didn't know what to think. I was afraid you were dead or hurt. I even had this moment of insanity when I thought you and Mason . . ." His voice trailed off.

"Mason? Ew!"

"Yeah, I couldn't see it either when rational thought returned. So I figured you were either dying or dead. When you walked through that door, it took everything in me not to let Mason see how glad I was that you were okay. But he's listening in so now he knows."

"I was so afraid that you'd be mad at me for not telling you sooner."

Leaning back, he studied my face and stroked his thumb along my cheek. "I was stunned. And the timing sucked. But I understand how hard it would be to tell me—to tell anyone—that you weren't a Shifter. I feel like I only just discovered you. Why would you trust someone you're just getting to know with your deepest secret?"

"I should have. I trust you with my life."

His eyes grew warm. "When I finally realized that banging my body against the bars wasn't going to do anything except create a cycle of bruising and healing, I started thinking about things. That bruise on your arm. It's not from Mason. It's from me. The day we wrestled."

I wanted to deny it, but if I had any chance at all of salvaging what remained of Connor's feelings for me, I had to be totally honest. I nodded. "I have one on my thigh, too. But it happens when someone is wrestling that aggressively. It's not as though you meant to bruise me."

"When you were standing in the media room—"

"It was too dark for me to see the empty seats. I was waiting for my eyes to adjust."

"When I kissed you and raced off in wolf form, you didn't follow because you couldn't."

I was embarrassed almost beyond enduring to admit it, but I murmured, "Yeah."

"Hey," he said tenderly.

It was only then that I realized tears were spilling from my eyes. I sniffed and wiped at the irritating wetness. "I'm sorry."

"I told you not to apologize for what you can't control."

"It's just that I hate being such a girl."

"I like that you're a girl." He tucked my hair back behind my ear. I hadn't bothered to braid it after the shower. "I like it a lot."

He kissed one corner of my mouth and then the other. His touch was as gentle as a butterfly alighting on a petal.

He brushed his lips over mine and then his tongue followed the same path. Warmth swirled through me.

"I don't care that you can't shift," he said quietly, before he settled his mouth over mine.

Easy enough to say when it was only the two of us in this small world, alone, not knowing what tomorrow might bring. But back in the real world, when he realized what an embarrassing freak I was, he wouldn't feel the same.

But I had tonight and I planned to make the most of it.

Death hovered in the shadows. Through the slit of the window, the barest of moonlight filtered in. I'd always drawn comfort from it, but tonight it was Connor offering me solace.

Within our prison, the mound of blankets softened the floor beneath us. One blanket covered us. Connor never bothered to put on the sweatshirt I brought him, so my fingers had the luxury of dancing over his bare chest.

"Don't be afraid, Brittany." Connor's voice was soft, gentle.

But how could I not be afraid? We both knew that tomorrow we might die. Facing death brought urgency to life. All the things we'd put off, all the things we hadn't dared to explore suddenly loomed before us as dreams that might never be fulfilled.

Connor held me close, his warm lips brushing over my temple. Beneath my palm I felt the steady pounding of his heart. How could his be so calm when mine was fluttering like a bird trapped in a cage?

He skimmed his mouth over my cheek. I heard him taking a deep breath, inhaling my fragrance. I pressed my face into the curve of his neck and took his unique scent into my lungs. Even here, inside this building where we were held captive, he smelled of the outdoors: evergreens, rich earth, sweet nectar, sharp foliage. He smelled of everything I love and more.

I'd waited so long to know the feel of his hands moving slowly over my back, urging me closer. I never wanted these moments to end.

"Don't be afraid," he whispered again.

Then the beast inside him that always hovered near the surface broke free and chased away the gentleness. He kissed me hungrily, desperately, as though with our wildness we could ward off the arrival of our enemy. I eagerly returned his kiss. I wanted to experience life with a passion I've never before known. I accepted that under normal circumstances we might not be tasting each other or running our hands over each other. But these circumstances weren't normal.

We'd been stripped of everything except the intense craving to experience everything we'd soon be denied.

"I love you, Brittany," he whispered.

Tremors cascaded through me. My heart pounded against my chest so hard that I was afraid my ribs might crack. He'd given me what I'd always longed for, what I absolutely didn't deserve.

Would his love turn to hate when he discovered that I'd betrayed him . . .

That I'd betrayed all the Shifters—that I'd given Mason the final thing he needed to complete his experiments?

FOURTEEN

The next morning I squinted against the sunlight. I'd fallen asleep with Connor's arms around me, but now I was alone. I had a moment of panic, fear shooting through me with the thought that somehow Mason had taken Connor, but when I sat up, I saw him standing in the middle of the cage, on all fours, staring at the window. He had no reason to hide his ability to shift now that Mason knew the truth. With a silly smile on my face, I simply sat there and admired him.

He was so incredibly gorgeous.

He swung his head around to look at me.

"Don't shift back yet," I said as I scooted over to him.

I buried my face, my fingers in his fur. I inhaled the scent of animal, the scent of Connor.

I rubbed his back. He emitted a low growl of approval.

"Do you know how beautiful you are?" I asked. "All the Shifters—in wolf form—are incredible but I've always thought you were the most stunning. I wanted so badly to have this."

He nuzzled my neck. I knew he was trying to comfort me. For all the closeness that had developed between us during this ordeal, I knew that we'd never be as close as Kayla and Lucas or Lindsey and Rafe. They had everything. Each other and the ability to shift. To always be in sync. To run through the woods together. To play in wolf form. To speak mind to mind. To embrace all that they were.

Connor and I would have only a portion of that. It was so not fair to him. I knew I would have to walk away when we were free.

He nudged my shoulder with his nose. As much as I hated to, I released my hold on him. He padded away. I didn't follow him with my eyes. I drew my knees up, wrapped my arms around my legs, and placed my chin on the support I'd created. I heaved a deep sigh. Could he truly ever understand the wonder of what he was?

I couldn't blame Mason for wanting it, because I wanted it, too.

Connor, now in human form, sat and put his arm around me. He was back in his jeans and now he was wearing the sweatshirt. "They're here," he whispered.

I jerked my head around, knowing he referred to the other Shifters. "So soon?"

He nodded.

"How many?"

"They have an entire army. Even all the adults they could muster are here. All we have to do is pretend it's business as usual in our little prison today—then tonight, freedom. And with any luck, the destruction of Bio-Chrome." He balled his fist. "I hope they get to us quick so we get a chance to join in the fight."

My stomach dropped. I wouldn't be able to fight like they did. I could imagine them all whispering in their minds, "Why isn't she shifting?"

As though reading my thoughts, Connor tucked his fingers beneath my chin and tilted my face toward his. "You have a mean roundhouse kick. You'll be an asset."

I forced myself to smile. "I'll do what I can."

He kissed me gently, more of a nibbling than anything passionate.

On the monitors where they were watching us, it probably just looked like we were snuggling. But in reality, my world was in the process of crumbling around me.

* * *

"So do you know anything at all about your father?" Connor asked.

We were sitting side by side while we waited. He was constantly combing his fingers through my hair as though he liked the feel of it as much as I enjoyed the feel of his fur. We were both restless, edgy, but for different reasons.

Connor was fighting not to keep shifting so he could communicate with the others. He knew Mason would get suspicious. I could also feel the tension thrumming through Connor. He was more than ready for the battle to begin.

Me? I was fighting not to shout out to Mason. My chance to be complete, to have the ability to shift was slipping away.

"His name is Antonio. She met him in France."

"Antonio? That's not very French sounding."

That hadn't even occurred to me when she told me. "Maybe he's not French. Maybe that's just where she met him. I didn't exactly hang around for details when she told me. I was so mad."

"I can't believe she never told you."

"I know, but that's so my mom. Sometimes it's like she thinks if she doesn't face things, they'll just go away."

"And that's so not you."

"Usually, but I wasn't good about facing the truth after I didn't shift. I was coming up with some excuses that were pretty out there."

He smiled. "I can imagine. I guess someone—the elders maybe—should have figured something out. Mates don't usually leave, you know, on account of that whole mate-for-life thing."

I shrugged. "There are always exceptions. Look at Rafe's dad. I'm not sure I ever saw him sober. And all those times Rafe came to school bruised. Some Shifters inherit the worst of human characteristics, I guess. I thought that was my dad."

"Everything's going to be all right, Brittany," Connor assured me and kissed my cheek.

I nodded. For him maybe. But I knew if I had to choose for things to be all right for just one of us—I'd choose Connor. Even if it meant losing him in the end.

He might have told me he loved me last night, but the emotion wouldn't stick once we were back among his kind. My dad had probably used the same words with my mother—but then he'd seen the reality of what she was. Or maybe Mom had become disgusted with what he wasn't. I wished now that I'd asked her more questions, but I'd been so mad at her for lying to me all these years. It felt as if she'd purposely tried to ruin my life.

"So when they took you out of here, what did it look

like? What can you remember of the layout?"

I put a little bit of space between us and began drawing an invisible map with my finger. I explained the route we'd taken to get to the living quarters. Everything I'd seen, heard, smelled, knowing even as I provided inadequate descriptions that they would have been far richer if I'd been a Shifter with keener senses.

"They didn't take me to the lab," I said quietly.

"That surprises me. I figured Mason would be dying to share his masterpiece in progress with you."

"I keep thinking about those little ferrets he turned into wolves."

"I'd bet money they died."

I jerked my head around. "You think?"

"Like I said before, I'm no biologist but Mason is messing with stuff he can't possibly understand."

"But do you think we are being selfish by not willingly sharing what we know, what you are? I mean, what if your ability to heal could really heal others?"

"Honestly, Brit? We have Shifters working in medical research because before the full moon, we're as vulnerable as anyone to disease or injury. I truly believe that if there was a way to bring our healing abilities to others they'd have made it happen. They understand how we work way better than Mason."

He was right. Shifters worked at all types of jobs in

cities around the world.

Our conversation dwindled to nothing as the hours dragged by and we became lost in thought regarding what we were each going to face. Connor was hoping Lucas would be able to find him quickly and release him so he'd be in the thick of battle. I was wondering if I could get to the lab in time after I was released.

All I wanted was one shot at the serum.

Mason didn't come to taunt us. No one brought us food or water.

"What if they've abandoned the lab?" I asked at one point.

"They're still here."

It was after darkness fell, when our prison was more shadows than light that all hell broke loose.

FIFTEEN

Connor and I were lying on our mound of blankets, holding each other close, listening intently, wondering what was going on when the lights above us came on for the first time—washing us in stunning brightness.

We both scrambled to our feet as the door opened. I expected to see Lucas coming to our rescue. Instead it was Mason striding in with an excitement in his step like a kid who'd just discovered that he had indeed gotten what he wanted for Christmas. In addition to his usual entourage, he had his father with him. Ethan was balancing a long case, using both hands, the way I imagined knights presented their swords to their liege lords. The whole procession was eerie—Mason was putting on a play and we were his audience.

I could feel the tension radiating from Connor. He was ready for a fight.

The entourage moved quickly to our cage. Wilson went to the side. There was a sizzling sound. Connor released a grunt and flopped without his usual grace to the floor. Only then did I see the stun gun Wilson had thrust between the bars.

"What did you do that for?" I demanded as I crouched beside Connor. I could see the shock and confusion in his eyes, him fighting to regain control of his body and mind.

"He'll be fine in a couple of minutes," Mason said. "Come on. I need you out now."

"All you did last time was threaten him, and he let you open the door. You didn't have to do this." I was furious.

"I was letting you back in then, not taking you out. You should see the video of how he reacted before—when he realized you were gone. The power he exhibited was amazing. I never grow tired of watching it. Now hurry. We have the formula ready to go and I want it tested tonight."

Leaning down, I pressed a kiss to Connor's cheek. I didn't even know if he'd be able to feel it. "I'm so sorry.

Please try to understand why I have to do this."

Then I crawled out through the door. Mason pressed the remote to quickly close it. Almost immediately I wished I was back on the other side with Connor. What was I doing? Mason's serum might kill me.

Mason snapped his fingers. Ethan stepped forward and opened the case to reveal two large syringes with a golden liquid filling them. Their actions were like a performance in a bad movie. I wondered if Mason had scripted their movements before they came in here. Probably. He seemed to take his role as the villain seriously.

I stared at those syringes. They looked so big.

"How do you know the dosage is right?" I asked.

"Educated guess."

I glared at him.

"I know more than your puny brain can imagine," he said impatiently.

"How do you know it's ready for human testing?"

"In addition to the ferrets, we've tested it out on a couple of other species with limited success. It's the consciousness factor that we talked about. And my father's here to handle any medical complications."

I looked over at Dr. Keane. He was smiling as though the experiment was already a triumph.

I glanced back at the cage. Connor was struggling to push himself to a standing position. With jerky movements he reached the front of the cage and wrapped his hands around the bars, probably to hold himself up more than anything. "What. You. Doing?"

He shook his head, no doubt trying to clear it.

"She didn't tell you?" Mason asked. "She is a keeper of secrets, isn't she? In exchange for me bringing her back to your little prison, she agreed to take the first injection."

Disbelief sharpened Connor's gaze. He shook his head.

"Oh, yes, my friend," Mason taunted. "I know it's difficult for you to understand but we humans will pay any price to possess your abilities."

With dramatic movements Mason removed the syringe from the case and arched a brow at me. "Taking it in your hip or thigh would probably be less painful."

I nodded. My mouth was dry but my palms were damp.

"Don't . . . do this, Brittany."

I jerked my head around. Connor had apparently shaken off the effects of the stun gun. I hesitated. "I'll be able to shift into a wolf. We'll be able to be together."

He shook his head, his eyes imploring me. "Don't let him change you into something I can't love."

I looked back at the syringe. I wanted so desperately what Mason was offering.

"If *you* love *me*, you won't do this," Connor said.

I slammed my eyes closed. *Not fair. So not fair.* When I opened my eyes, I could see that Mason was losing his patience. Suddenly everything in my world tilted. I could have what I'd always dreamed of being, but only if I was willing to give up what I'd always dreamed of holding.

I backed up until I hit the cage. Through the bars, Connor's arms came around me with strength and purpose.

"I changed my mind, Mason," I said.

"Too bad. Wilson, hold her."

Wilson started toward me.

"Touch her and you're dead," Connor said, and even though he was trapped in a cage, the threat in his tone made Wilson halt.

"Mason, it won't do any good to force me," I stated calmly, even though my heart was racing. "I won't will myself to change so you won't know if it works or not."

His expression took on that mulish look I'd seen before. "Ethan!" he barked.

Ethan stepped back. "No way, man. I thought we were doing this for medical research. I don't want to go furry."

"Coward," Mason spat. "Fine, I wanted to go first anyway."

The call of the wild—a long, deep pitched howl—echoed around us.

Mason arched a brow at me. "Sounds like you didn't tell me everything, Brittany. But I should have expected it. You werewolves own the nearby forest, don't you? It doesn't matter. I can use this opportunity to test my fighting instincts."

"Wilson, Johnson, get out there! Stop them from getting inside," Dr. Keane ordered.

When they were gone, Dr. Keane said, "Son, you should think about this."

"I have, Dad. It's all I've thought about since I learned their kind existed." Before anyone could react, Mason lifted his shirt and jabbed the syringe into his hip, pressing down on the plunger. I watched that golden liquid disappear.

He tossed the spent syringe on the floor. "So what do I do? Just think wolf."

"Just think wolf," Connor scoffed.

I figured he offered the advice because he didn't think the serum was going to work, so where was the harm in cooperating now? Besides, we were about to be rescued.

Mason tore off his shirt. He was reaching for his shoes when he suddenly released a high-pitched scream, doubled over, and dropped to the floor. "God, it hurts!"

"Did Devlin forget to mention that when he told you about us?" Connor asked. "The first shift for a male is excruciating. Let me out of here and I'll help you through it."

Mason rolled over and pushed himself to all fours. He glared at Connor. "I don't need your help."

Part of me felt sorry for him.

"You don't know what you're unleashing," Connor told him, and I felt the tension radiating from him.

And then Mason did start to shift, but nothing about it was beautiful. Everything about him began to get distorted and furry. He wasn't turning into a wolf, he was remaining a man—one with odd-looking limbs, facial features, and fur.

Ethan and Tyler raced for the door.

Dr. Keane cursed as he opened his bag and pulled out another syringe. "I'm going to put you under."

"No!" Mason yelled, but it was more growl than human voice. There was a wildness in his eyes, but it wasn't that of a true wolf.

I frantically searched around for a weapon, for something to free Connor. I spotted the remote to the door on the floor. I'd been so absorbed watching Mason that I hadn't even realized he'd dropped it. I snatched it up and pointed it toward the cage door. Before it was completely open, Connor had shifted and was coming out, snarling at Mason. But Mason was no threat to him. He couldn't control his grotesque limbs.

I looked at Dr. Keane. "He's not going to survive."

"He'll survive. I'll make sure of it."

I looked at the pitiful, howling thing rolling in agony on the floor.

"You need to get your people out of here." I grabbed Mason's discarded shirt and took the keycard out of the pocket. Then I was running for the door, Connor loping along beside me. I swiped the card through the reader and pushed the door open.

Then Connor and I were racing toward freedom.

It was chaos with people trying to escape and Shifters in wolf form chasing them out. Although it didn't appear that they were intent on harming them. It was more like they were herding them toward the exits. I guessed the guardians had decided on no collateral damage unless necessary. I wasn't surprised. Even in wolf form, they retained their humanity.

I spotted a sign for the lab and veered off down the hallway. Connor stayed with me, and I knew he'd shifted into wolf form to serve as my guardian. He had no weapon other than his powerful bite and his strength, but it would be enough.

The lab was empty except for two monkeys. I wondered where the other animals were that they'd been testing. Had they set them free in the forest? Or had they died?

I released the monkeys from their cages and ushered them into the hallway where their survival instincts took over. I heard glass breaking. When I looked back, Connor was leaping up on tables and knocking off equipment. I returned to help him. If they imploded the building, it would all get crushed anyway, but better to destroy it before anyone decided to take a dangerous souvenir.

When we were finished, we headed back out. Now more wolves than people were scattering through the building. Every now and then a wolf would stop to stare—I knew it was looking at me, wondering why I hadn't shifted.

And the speculations were spreading.

Then I saw a wolf with a familiar brownish red coat stop and look at me with sorrow reflected in its eyes. I ruffled my mom's fur as I raced by.

Eventually Connor directed me—with gentle nudges— outside. I didn't know exactly what the plan was, but I knew he did, that he was communicating with the others. I also knew that he wanted to be in the thick of things, but I was a deterrent. No matter how much I wanted it, I'd never be the best mate for him. I'd always be holding him back.

Once outside, I saw many of the wolves near the trees. They began disappearing in pairs, and when they returned they were in human form and dressed. I looked down at Connor. "I didn't think to bring your clothes."

He licked my hand and sat. I dropped down beside him and wrapped my arms around him, burying my face in his fur.

"You both okay?" a deep voice asked.

I looked up at Lucas. Kayla stood beside him. I forced myself to smile. "Yeah. What's the plan?"

"All of the humans are out of the building. A couple of tough-looking dudes put up a fight, but they're the only casualties. The rest seemed happy to just leave. Now we've got guys in there preparing it so we can bring it down."

"The people who left. They might have proof of our existence. They had video of Connor shifting," I told him.

"Yeah, we know. Connor told us, but I think we confiscated all the evidence."

I nodded. "Right. This morning." When he was in wolf form. "I guess he told you . . . everything."

"He had to. The pack comes first."

I tightened my fingers on Connor's fur. "I know. But even without evidence people are going to talk."

"Sure they will. But no one will believe them."

"I hope you're right."

"If I'm not, we'll deal with it. We've really done all we

can for tonight. Connor, I have some extra clothes if you want to shift back," Lucas said.

Connor lay down and put his head in my lap. I ruffled his fur, leaned over, and kissed the bridge of his nose. "I'll be okay."

"I'll stay with her," Kayla said.

He rolled his eyes to look at me.

"Seriously, I'm okay," I said.

He licked my chin and I smiled. "Go shift. I'd rather have a real kiss."

He headed off with Lucas, and Kayla sat beside me. She put her arm around my shoulders. "I'm so sorry. When I heard you weren't a Shifter—my heart just broke for you. You always worked so hard to prepare for it."

I shrugged. "I wanted it so badly, Kayla. I was going to take the serum, but in the end I just couldn't do it."

"Connor said Mason's dead."

"Yeah, he couldn't have survived what he was going through. It was horrible. It's like he was caught within the transformation. Not quite man, not quite beast."

"We didn't find him," Kayla said.

"His father probably took him out. He said he was going to try to save him, but I don't think there's any way that he could have."

"Didn't see Dr. Keane either."

"There were a lot of people in there—and a lot of

218

chaos. Do you think you may have missed them?"

"I guess it's possible."

"When Connor gets back, we can see if he wants to go looking for him. I think Mason is a smell he'll never forget."

"Lucas and I could probably find him. We should go looking for him. Just to be sure."

We sat in silence for several minutes. I stared at the building, not wanting to look into the eyes of anyone else. I didn't want to see pity or sympathy or disgust.

"Baby?"

I turned my head to the side. "Mom—"

"I know you're not a baby," she said, as she knelt beside me. "But you'll always be my baby. I'm so sorry I never told you the truth."

"It's okay, Mom."

I didn't know who reached for whom first but suddenly we were hugging each other tightly and I could barely breathe. Mostly because I was crying. Mom was crying, too, and the more she cried, the harder she squeezed me. I guessed when I really needed her, she *was* there for me.

Finally, I drew back and inhaled deeply. "I'm having too many girly moments."

Mom smiled and tucked my hair behind my ear. "You always thought you had to be tough."

"So what was he like—my father?"

"Listen, I'm going to leave you two alone," Kayla said.

Mom brushed her hand in the air. "Oh, you can stay. You should hear this. You, too, Lindsey. You can stop hovering back there."

"You smelled her," I said.

"Of course," Mom said as though it was nothing, then embarrassment touched her features as she realized I would never have the ability to distinguish individuals simply by their scent. "Brit—"

"It's okay, Mom. You can't stop being who you are, and I need to learn to be and accept who I am."

"I didn't want to disturb you," Lindsey said as she knelt in front of me.

I reached out and hugged her quickly. Long hugs seemed to generate tears. "Thanks for holding my secret."

"Hey, anytime, although it might be better if people didn't find out I knew."

"Right." She'd made a grave error in judgment putting me before the pack. I'd never forget her for it, though.

I turned back to Mom. "So, my dad?"

She pressed her hand to her heart. "Oh, Brittany. I hardly know where to begin. It was after my full moon. Michael and I had decided we weren't destined mates. We were simply friends. We went our separate ways, and I was feeling restless, so I went to Europe. Then I met Antonio. He was from Spain. He was the most handsome man. And he had the most delicious accent, the most beautiful eyes. Your eyes. And he was so romantic." She nudged her shoulder against mine. "We actually met in Brittany, France. Which is why I named you Brittany. We toured Europe together. I've always heard that when you meet your mate, it's like a kick to the gut. How unromantic."

I smiled, remembering saying something similar to Connor.

"But falling in love," my mom said dreamily, "is wonderful. It happens over time. He'll say something or do something and your heart just tightens."

I thought of Connor and all the times he'd made me smile or laugh or grow warm with desire.

"But he left you. Was it because you were a Shifter?" I asked.

Mom shook her head. "No, I never told him. I didn't have the courage to tell him."

I could so relate to that.

"I loved Antonio. Still do. He was the one for me. But I knew he could never accept what I was. Then I realized I was pregnant," Mom continued. "I wanted you raised among our kind, so I came back here.

"I know you were always disappointed that I wasn't one of the legendary Dark Guardians, but I was always a mother first. I don't regret it." She cradled my cheek. "I don't want you to regret it."

"I don't. I might have understood if you'd told me."

"And you might not have. It was my burden to carry. I mean, really, when do you tell your child that you were a rebel in your youth? Might give her ideas."

She made me smile. She'd always been able to make me smile. "I love you, Mom."

Winking at me, she squeezed my hand and nodded. I figured she thought anything more would result in additional tears. We'd never been big on tears.

I didn't smell him. I didn't hear him. But I knew he was there. I twisted around and smiled at Connor. "Hey."

"Hey." He sat behind me and put his arms around me. "Hi, Ms. Reed."

"Hello, Connor." She patted my arm. "Think it's time for me to go find some folks closer to my age. I brought the car. It's parked about ten miles from here. Find me if you want a lift home."

I figured she was the only Shifter who had arrived in a car, but then she was the only one with a human daughter.

"I'll see." I didn't know yet what my plans were. For all I knew, the elders would have me placed under house arrest for impersonating a Shifter.

"Okay!" Lucas yelled. "No one is left in the building.

Everyone stay back. They're ready to demolish the building." He raced toward us. Kayla met him halfway.

Lindsey wandered over to where Rafe was waiting for her.

Connor and I stood up to have a better view.

The series of explosions went off in a timed sequence and the building crumbled into a pile of debris and dust. Somehow after all we'd faced, it seemed . . . anticlimactic.

After the vaporous clouds settled, Lucas walked back over to us. "I'm going to send Guardians out to search for Mason and Dr. Keane. Their underlings I'm not too worried about. But the Keanes, we need to find. We can take them to Wolford, hold them prisoner there until the elders decide what to do with them."

"I'll help you search in a minute," Connor said. "I need to take care of something first."

Lucas nodded as though he knew what that something was. I was afraid I might, too. That something was me.

My suspicions were confirmed when Connor turned to me. "We need to talk."

I nodded. Yeah, we did.

Taking my hand, he led me away from the others. We walked along silently. On the horizon, the moon was leaving its quarter phase. They hadn't waited for the dark of the moon. Our being captured had sped up their plans, but in the end, it seemed to have all worked.

I wasn't convinced we'd seen the last of Bio-Chrome but no one else had seemed as obsessed as Mason and Dr. Keane—so maybe we were in the clear. We could always hope, but continue to prepare for the attack. I liked to think that the others were truly in it for the good of mankind, even if their methods were questionable.

We were at the edge of a clearing near an abundance of trees when Connor finally stopped and turned to face me.

"Were you serious about wanting to be Mason's guinea pig?" he asked.

"He wasn't going to return me to the cage. So we made a deal. If he returned me, I'd take the first injection."

"Why?"

"Because I wanted to be with you. And I wanted to be a Shifter so bad. I wanted to shift. I wanted to be beautiful."

"You're already beautiful."

"Oh, Connor." His words made me happier than I thought I could ever be. But I needed to explain that it was so much more. "You can't understand how much I wanted it. It's hard to let that dream go. To know I'll never—" I reached up and rubbed his bristly cheek. "It won't work with us if I can't shift."

"We can make it work."

"Be realistic, Connor. You can shift and be home by dawn."

"Or I could ride home with your mother."

I released a strangled laugh. "Yeah, that'll always be your number one choice."

"I'm not saying there won't be difficulties, but we could work them out. Besides, shifting is overrated."

With a smile, I pressed my face into the center of his chest. His arms came around me. Was I being a silly dreamer to imagine that we might be able to make this work?

Placing his knuckles beneath my chin, he tilted my face up. "I told you not to take the injection if you loved me," he said. "Does that mean you love me?"

"I've loved you for a long time. I wanted to die thinking about you and Lindsey beneath a full moon."

"You can walk away from those feelings?"

"If I have to. You deserve a *mate*. I don't know if I can ever truly be a mate."

Shaking his head, he gave me a soft grin. "I don't know if I've ever known anyone as strong as you."

His mouth found mine with unerring accuracy. I wanted to believe that it wasn't so much because he could see in the darkness, but because of something stronger. A bond between us. My mom had talked about falling in love. I couldn't deny that I'd fallen in love with Connor. He'd said he loved me.

Why was I so afraid to trust the intensity of his feelings? What if one day he looked across a room and felt that jolt that signaled he'd just found his true mate? How would he feel then if he was stuck with me?

He pulled back. "Do you smell that?"

"Monique? I'm still wearing her clothes."

"No . . . it's"—he inhaled deeply—"Mas—"

A growl echoed through the air and a heavy weight thudded into us, taking us to the ground.

It *was* Mason. His shape was more man than wolf. He was covered in fur. His face was a caricature of a wolf's. It was as though when shifting it hadn't been able to decide exactly what it should be.

His long fingernails cut grooves down my arm. I yelled, kicked, maneuvered out from beneath him. Connor made his escape as well. He was ditching his clothes as quickly as possible, while I began looking for a weapon. I'd felt Mason's strength. I didn't think my wrestling moves were going to take him out.

He leaped on my back, crushing me back to the earth. He'd misjudged, though, and overshot his mark because when we landed I was tucked up beneath his chest, which made me beyond reach of his snapping teeth. Growling and snarling, he leveraged himself so he could get to me.

It was all I needed to position myself so I could toss him off. I scrambled away.

I heard another growl, this one more menacing, more controlled. I looked back in time to see Connor diving for Mason. They were both brutal in their attempts to take the other down. But there was a madness to Mason that I wasn't sure we could defeat.

I found a branch on the ground. It was sturdy but too long. I grabbed both ends, put my foot in the middle and jerked up. It snapped in two, giving me what I wanted: a stick the length of both my hands—a stick with a pointed end.

I hurried over to where Connor and Mason were locked in battle. They were snarling at each other, snapping their teeth. Connor was on top but he couldn't get close enough to the jugular because Mason's absurdly long arms kept him beyond reach.

Bouncing on the balls of my feet, I prepared myself. Then I swung my leg around and knocked Connor off. Immediately I went to my knee and plunged the stake through Mason's heart.

He wasn't a vampire, but a stake through the heart will kill practically anything.

SIXTEEN

It was sad that in death Mason reverted back to his human form. He looked so innocent, almost sweet. No harshness, no cynicism, no obsession.

Before Connor shifted back, he had howled into the night but it wasn't a howl of triumph. It was a call to the others. That he'd taken no satisfaction in Mason's death made me love him all the more.

I didn't know where Kayla had found the blanket but she knelt beside Mason and draped it over his still form. With gentle fingers she combed back his hair. "Find peace, Mason."

Earlier in the summer they'd been friends. It occurred

to me that it was his obsession with the Shifters more than the formula that had destroyed him.

And that left me to wonder if I was any different. Was I letting my obsession with not being a Shifter destroy what I might have with Connor? Or was I truly being unselfish in my desire to let him go?

"Found Dr. Keane—or what's left of him," Rafe said, as he and Lindsey joined the group. "Looks like he was Mason's first victim."

I wanted to believe that Mason hadn't realized he was killing his father, that every aspect of him that was human had disappeared until he was only a beast that he couldn't control.

"Poor Mason," Kayla said. "I like to think that in the beginning he did want to do something good for mankind. Our healing properties are miraculous."

"He got greedy," Lucas said, slipping his arms around her. "We can lay him and Dr. Keane to rest at Wolford."

She glanced back at him and smiled. "Thank you."

Holding me close, Connor whispered, "Are you going to be all right? I know the first kill is never easy."

"He would have killed us if he could have."

"Still doesn't make it easy."

"Sorry I kicked you."

"I'm not. I couldn't have held him off much longer."

I nestled my face into the curve of his shoulder. "I want to go home."

My mother hadn't yet left so Connor and I found her. The three of us hiked to her car. When Connor and I started to get in the back she said, "Hey, I'm not a chauffeur. You drive me." She tossed him the keys.

She sat in the back while I sat in the passenger seat. I think she forced that arrangement so Connor and I wouldn't be snuggling in the backseat. Mom was okay making out with a Spaniard when she was seventeen, but she didn't want her daughter doing anything of the sort.

Still, Connor held my hand, his thumb sometimes circling my palm, and I wondered what he was thinking during those moments. I still didn't know what I was going to do about us. But I was too exhausted to think clearly. I figured he was as well.

When we got to the house, Connor pulled into the drive. I tried to get out of the car, but it was like my body didn't want to work. It had grown heavy, weighted down. Or maybe it was just so incredibly tired that it could no longer send messages to my brain.

"Brittany?" Mom prodded.

"I'm fine." An easy enough lie to pull off since Connor had come around, opened the door for me, took my hand, and pulled me out.

I'd forgotten that he was raised in a traditional, well-mannered family that did things like that. I didn't know what I was thinking to fall for him. We had nothing in common.

With his arm behind me, he practically propelled me up the walk to the door. Mom opened it, then turned around and held up her hand like a traffic cop. "Five minutes."

She closed the door, leaving us on the dark porch. The light suddenly came on.

"Has she always been like that?" Connor asked.

"There's never been a guy in my life before. She's probably making up for lost chaperone time or something. She'll settle down." I had to shove out each word.

He trailed his fingers along my cheek. "Call me if you need me."

He bent his head and kissed me so gently that I almost didn't feel it. Then he opened the door and pushed me inside. "Tell your mom she owes me some rollover minutes."

I released a light laugh as he pulled the door closed. I stood there for the longest time, envisioning him walking home. He didn't live that far. How many times in high school had I detoured by his house after school hoping to catch a glimpse of him?

I might have stayed there all night if Mom hadn't come over and put her arms around me.

"Come on. I prepared you a bubble bath."

"Will you burn Monique's clothes?" I asked as she led me toward the bathroom. "I never want to see them again."

"Consider it done."

As I got undressed, I noticed that I'd collected a few more bruises. I had a couple of scrapes but nothing that would scar. The scratches I received when Mason raked his claws over my arm were another matter. They might scar.

When I sank into the hot water, I thought I'd found heaven. I didn't remember anything feeling so good—except lying against Connor. Even on a concrete floor, curled up against him was wonderful.

There was a knock on the door. "Brittany, can I come in?"

"Sure, Mom."

She handed me a glass of white wine.

"I'm not twenty-one," I reminded her.

"Sometimes, my dear, you're older than your birth certificate claims."

I took a sip. It was sweet and smooth going down my throat. It sent a warm lethargy through my veins.

Mom knelt beside the tub. "Relax now. I'm going to wash your hair."

"Mom, you haven't washed my hair since I was about six."

"I still remember how."

She poured water over my hair, added shampoo, and began to massage my scalp. I thought I might just sink below the water and sleep forever.

"So," she began. "You and Connor."

That was subtle.

"Maybe. I don't know, Mom."

"I like him."

I smiled. "You mean I got the guy thing right on the first try?"

"It happens."

"Was my dad your first?"

"Mm-huh."

"You've never seen him again?"

"In my dreams. Every night."

"Is that enough, Mom?"

"For me. But I wish more than that for you."

I wished more than that for me, too.

After my bath, my hair and skin practically squeaked. I applied some antibiotic cream to the scratches on my arm and bandaged it up. I slipped on soft cotton shorts and a tank, said good night to Mom at my bedroom door—unable to remember the last time we'd actually taken a moment to say it—then crawled into my bed. My body sank into the mattress.

I tried to close my mind but the events of the past

several days were running through it like a slide show. I'd see Connor fighting the cougar, the shock on his face when he learned the truth about me, Mason holding up the syringe . . .

The stake. The way it had felt going through his chest—

I wanted to concentrate on the good moments: Connor kissing me, holding me, defending me . . .

But the uglier images kept shutting them out. My chest grew tight and I felt a building up of tears behind my eyes. I felt as though I was strangling.

I heard a knock on my window. Glancing over, I could see a shadow. I scrambled out of bed and pulled back the curtain. Connor was balanced on a tree branch. I opened the window. "What are you doing?"

He crawled in through the window. "I've slept with you so many nights that now I can't sleep without you."

"Seriously."

"I am serious." He touched my cheek. "I just thought you might need holding tonight."

Tears flooded my eyes. I shook my head. "I'm not going to cry, I'm not going to cry, I'm not—"

He lifted me in his arms and carried me to the bed. "It's all right to cry, Brit. It's been a hell of a few days."

He laid me on the bed, slipped in beside me, and took me in his arms. The tears wouldn't stop, which really made me mad because they were making my nose go all stuffy and I was finding it more difficult to inhale his scent.

"You smell so good," I said.

"I showered. Best shower I've ever had."

I slid my hand up into his hair. The ends were still wet and the strands curled around my fingers.

"I'm so glad it's all over," I whispered.

"Me, too. Cry all you want, Brit. It'll be our secret."

While he rubbed my back, I cried long and hard. Loud sobs were muffled as I buried my face against his chest. All the fear, the terror, the grief from the past few days just built up and flowed out. The times when I'd pretended to be brave had been the hardest of all. The times when I'd tried not to let Connor see how terrified I was of what they might do to him. Or of what he'd think when he learned the truth about me.

I cried until his shirt was damp and my eyes were swollen.

I thought I was still weeping when I fell asleep.

The knock on the door woke me.

"Okay, you two, breakfast is ready."

I gasped. I was still in Connor's arms. How had—

"Don't be so surprised, baby. I have a keen sense of smell."

I cringed. I knew she'd called me baby just to irritate me.

Hearing her footsteps on the stairs, I dared to tilt my head back. Connor smiled down on me.

"Sleeping with a babe *and* breakfast. What a deal."

I nipped his chin. "Thanks for last night."

"I've been there, Brittany. My first kill was a bear. God, he was magnificent, but he was attacking a camper." I could see in his eyes the sadness he was feeling with the memory. "He'd just kinda gone crazy. He wouldn't run off."

I knew humans probably couldn't understand the grief Shifters felt over the death of an animal, but they were part animal as well, and they grieved at any loss of life.

"Does it get easier?" I asked.

"No, but I don't think I'd want it to. If killing came easily then I'd be like the men my father prosecutes."

I touched his cheek. I almost told him again that I loved him, but I wondered if repeating—confirming—my feelings would make it harder when the time came for us to separate. Instead I kissed him.

Then we went down to the kitchen.

"Better not have been anything other than sleep going on in that room last night," Mom said as we joined her at the table.

"Mom!"

"There wasn't," Connor assured her.

With a nod, she passed him the biscuits. I couldn't remember the last time my mom cooked breakfast. We both usually just took care of ourselves.

"You don't have to make things up to me, Mom."

"I always cook when we have company. Don't expect this tomorrow."

"The pancakes are delicious, Ms. Reed," Connor said.

I narrowed my eyes at him and mouthed, "Suck-up." He winked at me.

"Thank you, Connor. So what are your intentions regarding my daughter?"

"Mom! God. That is so . . . a hundred years ago. People don't ask that anymore."

"Maybe they should."

Connor laughed. He was having entirely too much fun. He started to say something, but the doorbell rang.

"I'll get it," Mom said, dropping her napkin on the chair and heading for the door.

"I'm so sorry," I said, with a roll of my eyes.

"Don't worry about it." He tapped his fork against his plate. "So what do you want my intentions toward you to be?"

"Connor, I—"

Mom walked in holding a black envelope. She was so pale that I thought maybe she'd left all her blood at the front door.

"Mom?"

She jumped, as though startled. "It's for you."

"Me?" I took it from her. My name was written in elegant gold script. I turned it over. It wasn't an envelope. It was a piece of paper with all four corners folded into the center and held in place with a wax seal of a snarling wolf. I opened it carefully and read what was written inside. Suddenly it was like all the air had been sucked out of the room. I grew dizzy.

"Brittany?" Connor said, covering my hand with his.

I looked at him, then at Mom, then back at him. "It's from the Council of Elders. It's a summons. Tomorrow they're holding a tribunal to determine my status as a Dark Guardian."

"They could have at least given her a few days to recover from the hell we went through," Connor said to his father. His father was a lawyer. I knew Connor planned to follow in his footsteps.

Now, though, he was pacing in his father's study. I'd never seen so many books in my life—except in a library.

But I was beginning to get accustomed to Connor's anger where injustice was concerned.

His father was sitting behind his desk. He looked so incredibly distinguished. I wondered if Connor would resemble him as he got older. "The elders don't usually put off the unpleasant."

"You can represent her," Connor said.

"Lawyers aren't allowed inside."

"So *what*—she has to face them alone?"

His father tapped an expensive-looking gold pen on his desk. "The tribunal will involve the Council of Elders and the Dark Guardians. They'll listen to the evidence and make a determination."

Connor looked at me where I was sitting in a chair by the window and smiled. "Then you've got nothing to worry about. If the Guardians—"

"Connor, your decision can't be based on emotion. It has to be made after listening to the facts and determining what is best for the pack. As a matter of fact, son"—he lifted a black envelope similar to what I'd gotten—"you're not to have any contact with her until after the tribunal. If you'd been home this morning, this would have already been delivered to you and you'd understand your responsibilities."

Averting his eyes, Connor crossed his arms over his chest. "Until I open it, I don't know exactly what it says."

"Be careful, son. If you go against the elders' wishes,

they'll ban you from the tribunal and then you'll be facing one of your own. They don't take well to insubordination. The Dark Guardians may be running around protecting us, but the elders control things and have the final say in all matters."

With my knees shaking, I got up, walked over to his father, and held out my hand. "May I have it?"

He arched a sandy blond brow at me but handed it over.

I took it to Connor. "There is nothing I've ever wanted more than I wanted to be a Dark Guardian." *Except you.* But it wouldn't be fair to him to tell him that. Not now. Not with what we were about to face—what we had to face separately. "You can't throw that away. Besides, I want you there tomorrow."

I could tell he was shocked by my words.

"I can make it through this thing if I can look over and see you. I draw strength from your presence. And if they determine that I can't be a Dark Guardian—and quite honestly I'd vote against me—I'll survive. So think about your vote. Your dad's right—it shouldn't be based on emotion. The pack comes first." I tucked the envelope behind his crossed arms.

As I walked out of the room, he didn't say a word. And I knew he'd be there tomorrow, doing his duty as a Dark Guardian, determining my fate.

SEVENTEEN

I wore black trousers, a black shirt, and a black jacket. I looked like someone preparing to go to a funeral. I just hoped it wasn't my own.

My mom wanted to come with me, but I felt as though there were some things I needed to face alone. This was one of them. I'd always known my actions—claiming to be a Shifter when I wasn't, sneaking into the treasures room, other lies and transgressions—came with consequences. Not to mention everything I'd told Mason. If anyone discovered the secrets I'd revealed . . .

I hadn't told them about my trip to the white and black room, its décor so eerily symbolic. Good and evil.

Connor didn't even know everything I'd told Mason, all that had transpired while I'd been away from him. But whatever my punishment was for any of my offenses, I was prepared to accept it. Given the choice, I knew I'd do them all again—especially the deals I'd made with Mason. To save Connor, I would have given up my life.

I drove Mom's car to Wolford. We were going to go car shopping this afternoon—regardless of this morning's outcome. Since she now had confirmation that I'd never be traveling on all fours, she'd decided I needed some wheels. I was okay with that.

Now I was waiting to be called into the council room. I paced in front of the door, trying not to think about what was going to happen on the other side. I'd prepared a little speech, but I thought I might hyperventilate before I could give it. It would be so much easier if they'd just let me wrestle for the right to remain a Guardian.

The door opened, and I swore it sounded like the report of a rifle.

Lucas came through looking as though his face had been set in stone this morning, and I realized this wasn't any easier for them than it was for me. Why hadn't I just faced the truth of my situation after the full moon? Why had I tried so hard to hide it? Secrets always came out.

"We're ready for you," he said solemnly.

With a nod, I followed him into the room and stood

in the designated spot. In front of me, the three elders sat at a table covered with a black cloth. Like judges, they wore black robes. Resting before Elder Wilde was a book I recognized—the book that housed the ancient text. So things were going to be pretty formal. I'd heard somewhere that in ancient days they'd thrown the guilty into a pit of real wolves. I was really hoping that wasn't one of the ancient rituals they clung to.

Behind them was a large flat-screen TV. I had a feeling that didn't bode well for me.

On either side of their table, at an angle, were two other long ones, also covered in black. Six guardians sat at one, five at the other. My stomach knotted up with the significance of the chair beside Connor being empty. I didn't know if I'd ever wanted to sit beside him as much as I did right at that moment. For the first time in ages, his hair looked as though a comb, instead of his fingers, had gone through it. He had no stubble whatsoever adding shadow to his face. Like all the other guardians, he was dressed in black. As handsome as he appeared, I missed the rough, don't-mess-with-me look that usually characterized him. My stomach fluttered just a bit as I envisioned him—polished and perfect—striding into a courtroom years from now.

Elder Wilde slammed a gavel on a slab of wood, and I jumped. I hadn't been this unnerved facing Mason. But then the only thing at risk had been my life. Right at that moment, I knew I could lose everything I treasured. Everything that made my life worth living.

"The tribunal will begin," he said in a deep, sonorous voice that echoed off the walls, and made me think the reverberations would hang around for generations. "Guardian Reed, you have been brought before this tribunal because of actions and failures to act that cause us great concern regarding your ability to effectively serve as a Dark Guardian, protector of our kind. Please step forward."

I did as instructed, three long steps that seemed to take forever to make.

He pushed the leather and gilded book toward me. "Do you swear on the ancient text to answer all questions truthfully?"

I placed my palm on the book. I'd touched it before but never had it felt so intimidating. "I do."

"Step back."

Again, I followed his orders. I knew now was not the time to be belligerent, even though I thought they were being a little too dramatic. It seemed to me this could be handled fairly quickly.

Are you a Shifter?

No.

You're outta here.

But the elders apparently thought things needed to be dragged out.

"Was the last full moon designated as your shifting moon?" Elder Wilde asked.

"It was."

"Did you face it alone?"

"I did."

"Did you shift?"

I darted a glance at Connor. He gave me a barely perceptible nod. It was enough to strengthen my resolve not to cower from the truth. "No."

"Did you tell Shifters that you did?"

I furrowed my brow. "I don't think I ever actually said I did, but I might have insinuated that I did."

"Are you a Shifter, Guardian Reed?"

Out of love and respect for my mother, and the choice she'd made, I lifted my chin as haughtily as I could. "No, I'm human."

Kudos for me. My voice didn't shake.

"Are you aware that only Shifters may serve as Dark Guardians?"

"Yes."

"You didn't think you needed to inform the elders of this . . . shortcoming?"

"I was ashamed."

"Did you enter the treasures room without permission

to look through the sacred ancient text?"

"Yes."

"Were you captured by Bio-Chrome?"

I'd so hoped that they wouldn't go there. My gaze jumped to the flat screen, before settling back on Elder Wilde. "Yes."

He gave a nod. Elder Mitchell twisted around in his seat and pointed a remote at the TV. It came on and in the next instant, Connor and I were back in the cage right after the cougar attack. I was holding him in my lap, yelling at Mason.

My first thought was that I looked terrible! My hair was a tangled mess, my eyes had a wildness in them, my face was smudged with dirt. How could Connor have stood holding me?

It was painful to hear me bargaining with Mason, even more painful to see Connor lying there so still and pale.

The scene abruptly cut to the white and black room. I was freshly showered. I looked like a traitor.

Standing in the council room now, I fought not to squirm as I watched Mason peppering me with questions that I answered in a flat, emotionless voice. My eyes even looked dead. Having to endure all this again was cruel and unusual punishment. Where was Amnesty International when I needed them?

The video rolled along until it reached the worst part of my ordeal.

"*Come on, Mason. Let me go back. I told you every-thing I know.*"

"*Everything?*"

"*Everything.*"

"*Then what do you have to bargain with?*"

I'd looked panicked when I thought I'd appeared so cool and in control. I could see my mind searching for something, anything. I knew by the slump of my shoulders when I found it. Then I straightened on that stupid white sofa.

"*At some point, you're going to need to test your serum or whatever it is on a human.*"

He grinned. "*Are you volunteering?*"

I swallowed. "*Yeah.*"

"*Let me make sure I have this right—if I take you back to the cage, when the serum is perfected, you'll will-ingly let me inject you with it?*"

"*Yeah, as long as you don't talk, because I'm really getting tired of hearing you talk.*"

"*I'll want a full report of everything you experienced, everything you felt.*"

"*You'll get it.*"

Watching the victorious grin of satisfaction that crossed Mason's face, I saw again on the screen what I'd recognized in that stupid room—I'd given Mason exactly what he'd wanted all along. A human guinea pig.

Thank goodness the TV suddenly went black. The torture was over. Everyone knew that my lying about being a Shifter was the least of my transgressions. I couldn't look at Connor. I just couldn't. I'd never wanted him to know exactly what had happened when I wasn't with him. I'd betrayed everything he and the Dark Guardians were fighting for. To protect their kind.

"Do you have anything to say in your defense for your flagrant disregard of our traditions and rules and your willingness to consort with the enemy?" Elder Wilde asked.

Consort? Who used words like that anymore? I opened my mouth—

"If it pleases the elders, I have something to say," Connor announced.

As one, the three elders turned their heads toward him. "It does please the elders, Guardian McCandless."

Connor stood, his gaze homing in on the elders like that of a predator who intended to intimidate its prey into surrendering. "I've known Brittany a long time." He shook his head. "No, I haven't *known* her. I've *seen* her. Working out, running. Taking campers into the wilderness. Not until we were captured by Bio-Chrome did I really get to *know* her. You've only watched a minuscule fraction of our time with Bio-Chrome. For days we were prisoners, left alone with no idea of what was going on. She never grew discouraged, she never complained. Sometimes she even made me laugh.

"She's courageous. They released a cougar on us to force us to shift. She couldn't. I did. But she didn't cower in the corner. She used her strength and a hell of kick to distract it so I could get the advantage.

"She's resourceful. When Mason attacked us in the forest, I shifted, but again, she couldn't. I had him pinned, but I couldn't finish him off. She kicked me—*kicked* me—off of him so she could get to him and impale him with a weapon she'd made.

"She's loyal. When they took her away and refused to bring her back, she made a deal with the devil to return to me, to our prison, so I wouldn't be alone. You just saw her interrogation. She didn't tell Mason anything that would have helped him, anything that was a true betrayal to us.

"Yes, we have the ability to shift into wolf form, but we are not wolves. It is our intelligence, our courage, and our willingness to put others first that separates us from the animals. No one is more dedicated to protecting the Shifters than Brittany. Whether or not she is a Dark Guardian, she is my mate. I declare her as such."

I heard a couple of gasps. The loudest of all was mine.

"Connor, no! You don't know what they'll decide. They could banish me, they could—"

His gorgeous blue eyes came to bear on me. "I don't care what they decide, Brittany. You told me that there was nothing you wanted more than to be a Dark Guardian. There's nothing I want more than I want you."

I felt the tears burning my eyes.

I will not cry. I will not cry.

"Connor, I lied. There is something I want more than to be a Dark Guardian. You."

He grinned with satisfaction. "I was hoping you'd feel that way. You're my mate—if you so choose."

For the flicker of a heartbeat it looked as though he doubted what my answer would be. I'd never wanted anything more. "I choose you."

His eyes held so much love, warmth, and pleasure that nothing else that was facing me this morning seemed important. They could kick me out, banish me, send me to the moon, and I'd be happy.

"Have you anything else to add, Guardian McCandless?" Elder Wilde asked.

"No, sir."

The elder nodded and Connor sat.

"Have you anything to say in your own defense, Guardian Reed?" Elder Wilde asked.

"I never meant to put anyone in danger. I truly thought

I could perform my duties even though I couldn't shift. But I also knew if I told the truth about my situation, that I wouldn't be accepted. I've only ever known life among the Shifters, so maybe I'm not quite as brave as Connor thinks. I didn't want to be kicked out. But I will accept the decision of the tribunal."

I released a deep breath. In the back of my mind, I thought I'd said too little, that there was more I should have said.

Elder Wilde held my gaze. "The question before the tribunal is whether or not, in light of your actions, you may serve as a Dark Guardian. Before we go any further, I have something to add. The answer you were seeking in the ancient text. I may have found it."

I couldn't have been more stunned if he'd suddenly announced he wasn't a Shifter either. "You didn't even know the question."

He gave me an indulgent smile. "I am the senior elder for a reason."

I wasn't even sure I knew the question anymore. So much had happened, and now I knew I'd never be able to shift, so he certainly hadn't found the secret to that dilemma. "All right. What's the answer?"

"First, answer me this: Are you ready to face your judgment?"

Swallowing hard, I nodded. "Yes, sir."

He folded his hands on the old leather book as though he had the ability to access its contents through osmosis. "The ancient text refers to a woman with the heart of a wolf, but the inability to shift. It says through her the humans and Shifters will unite. Perhaps you will become that woman, Brittany Reed, perhaps not. But the Council of Elders cannot deny you have the heart of a wolf. It is up to the Dark Guardians to determine whether or not you are worthy to stand beside them. As you are his declared mate, Guardian McCandless may not vote."

I saw Connor's jaw clench. But since that was the only reaction he exhibited, I decided he'd known what his declaration would cost him.

"We will take the vote," Elder Wilde said.

Lucas stood. "Worthy."

Kayla. "Worthy."

Rafe. "Worthy."

Lindsey. "Worthy."

Those four I'd expected.

Daniel stood. "Worthy."

I was halfway there.

Five more guardians stood. "Worthy."

I knew Dark Guardians didn't cry, but all the blinking in the world didn't stop a solitary tear from rolling down my cheek. I let it go, didn't try to swipe it away, because I didn't want to bring attention to it.

"The decision has been made. Brittany Reed, you will remain a Dark Guardian."

My knees grew so weak that I thought I was going to have to sit down. "Thank you, sir. I won't let the Shifters down."

He smiled. "I never thought you would, Brittany. You should also know that the elders have always known you didn't have the ability to shift."

I didn't know whether to be angry or stunned. "But you tried to find me a mate."

"So you wouldn't be alone when you learned the truth."

"Why didn't you just tell me?"

"The transformation involves more than the body. It is a journey of the heart, soul, and mind. You still had roads to travel in order to arrive here."

"That morning in the archive room, you were setting me up."

"We were testing you."

I had a feeling they were still testing me, so I clamped my mouth shut.

With a smile, as though he'd read my thoughts, he said, "This tribunal is now ended." He brought his gavel down with a loud rap.

Chairs scraped back, and I knew the Guardians were going to start coming over to welcome me back, but there was only one I wanted to be with. He met me halfway, put his arms around me, lifted me up, and laughed. It was such a warm, joyous sound.

"Are you sure, Connor? Are you sure you want me for your mate?"

"I've never been more sure of anything."

"But with me you'll never experience that first shifting with a mate, that bond that is created."

His eyes heated, but his voice was teasing. "There are other firsts that we'll experience together, other ways to create bonds."

Then he kissed me—in front of the other Guardians and the elders—but I didn't mind if the whole world knew. At long last, I had my mate. But more than that, I had Connor.

EIGHTEEN

That night we all met at the Sly Fox: Lucas, Kayla, Rafe, Lindsey, Connor, and me.

We were sitting in a horseshoe-shaped booth, eating pizza, and drinking root beer. For the first time in a long time, I really felt included, part of the pack. The tension I'd felt with Lindsey for much of the summer because of her relationship with Connor had melted away. And I was looking forward to getting to know Kayla better. She was going to start jogging with me in the mornings.

"You really took a chance there disqualifying yourself," Lindsey said to Connor. "What if the vote had been tied?"

"My dad advised me that if I didn't want her banned from being a Dark Guardian then I had to convince them that I thought she was worth making sacrifices for. Giving up a vote? Small stuff."

He reached for his mug of root beer and his newest tattoo peeked out from behind his sleeveless shirt. I skimmed my fingers over it. That afternoon, while I'd been out shopping for cars with my mom, he'd had the tattoo bearing Lindsey's name removed. I didn't want details because I was fairly certain it had been a painful process that involved shifting to heal. Then he'd had my name interwoven in a Celtic symbol inked onto his left shoulder. Because the ink is injected into the second layer of skin, while the wound that tattooing creates does heal during shifting, the ink remains in the original design in which it was applied.

"I'd always heard that a Shifter male had to bear the name of his first choice forever," I said.

"Urban legend," he said, as he gave me a quick kiss.

"The whole point was that guys were supposed to be discouraged from making rash decisions regarding their mates," Lindsey said.

"Yeah, well, maybe the girls need to give it a little more thought, too," Connor teased her.

"Can't argue with that." She snuggled against Rafe.

"So tell us about your car," Kayla said.

I couldn't stop the bright smile from forming. "Mom said it needed to reflect my wild outlook, so she bought me a red Mustang."

"Whoa!" Kayla exclaimed. "Way to go, girlfriend. You'll be the coolest girl at school in the fall."

"Oh, I can walk to school. Mostly I'll use it to go see Connor at college. It should get me there pretty fast."

"You better drive slowly," Connor warned. "No accidents."

I knew he was worried because I didn't possess his ability to heal. Our—their—kind did tend to be reckless because only a fatal wound was ever really a problem. But humans lived to ripe old ages, too. I was going to have to look for a new doctor, though, since the only ones Shifters usually went to were pediatricians. Kids didn't have the ability to shift and heal either.

"Hey!" A pitcher of root beer thudded onto our table. "Glad things worked out for you."

I smiled at Daniel. "Thanks for your vote this morning."

"I never hold a grudge when a girl turns me down."

"I didn't exactly turn you down."

"Grab a seat," Connor offered.

"We're going to have to find you a mate," Kayla said to Daniel.

"Well, let's not go with the old draw-a-name-from-a-hat technique. That didn't work out too well," he said, grinning.

I peered over at Connor. "Thought you said it was a bowl."

"Does it matter?" he asked, as he put his arm around me.

"No." I snuggled up against him, always amazed by how perfectly we fit together.

"So?" Lucas prodded. "Anyone up for a two-legged run in the moonlight?"

NINETEEN

The night sky was brilliant with so many stars that it was as though someone had casually tossed diamonds onto blackness. The full moon was bright and appeared to be close enough to kiss the earth. As I knelt on the dew-covered grass, I couldn't see a single cloud. Taking a deep breath, I could smell the wildflowers that coated the ground. Nearby the trees rustled in the breeze while I waited.

I was in a place that Shifters simply referred to as the waterfall. It was possibly the most romantic place within the national forest. I could hear the nearby water rushing over the cliffs and crashing into the pool below. Behind the curtain of water was a cavern where we stored essentials for those rare times when someone needed a sanctuary. But most of all, the males brought their mates here for their first shifting. Afterward they'd go to the cave to spend their first night together.

But before tonight, Connor and I had already slept curled around each other. We'd awoken several mornings in each other's arms.

What we were doing tonight was more symbolic. Connor wanted to share a ritual with me that neither of us had experienced before. And while it wouldn't be exactly what every other Shifter couple went through, what he'd planned seemed perfect for us.

I watched as the moon rose higher in the night sky. Moonlight washed over me. I tingled, but it wasn't the moon's work that caused the pleasant sensations. It was simply the result of me awaiting the arrival of my true mate.

When the moon reached its zenith, I lowered my gaze to the trees that lined the perimeter of the clearing. The brownish golden wolf waited at its edge. The moonlight glistened over his fur as he stepped out.

He was powerful and magnificent as he prowled toward me, his eyes holding mine. In Connor's eyes, I saw all the love he held for me.

When he stopped before me, I buried my fingers in

his fur and pressed him against me. I hoped he heard the pounding of my heart and understood that his nearness made it beat faster. That when I was with him, I always felt as though I was running, always experienced the heady rush of an amazing workout.

He licked my chin and I laughed.

Reaching over I picked up the black cloak that the guy usually wore while he helped his mate welcome her first transformation. I draped it over the wolf, and in the blink of an eye, the wolf had retreated and Connor was kneeling before me.

For most Shifters the bonding happened when human became wolf. For us, it happened when we were both in human form. Like my ancestors, we'd taken the human route toward finding a mate: We'd fallen in love.

"I'd once told Lindsey that I thought Shifters were the most beautiful when they were in wolf form. I think she thought I was crazy. She said that for her there was no difference. I didn't understand." I touched his cheek. "I've always thought you were gorgeous in wolf form, but now I prefer you like this."

Turning his head, he kissed my palm. "I'll only revert to wolf when I have to—to protect the pack."

"Do you think there will still be dangers? Mason is gone. I heard Bio-Chrome has no more funding. Investors probably realized the research was too dangerous after what happened to Mason and Dr. Keane. Surely we'll be safe now."

"There are always dangers for us, Brittany. Dark Guardians will always be needed."

As he brought me to my feet, I didn't want to think about the enemies who might rise up against us or the threats they would bring.

"I don't resent that you can shift, Connor. You can be a wolf anytime you want. I'll still love you."

He flashed a grin just before he kissed me. His lips were warm and tender as he drew me close.

I liked to think as the moon watched us that it approved.